THE TALES OF [illegible]

BOOK 2

# THE SLAVES OF MAZARON

COLSON ROSA

THE SLAVES OF MAZARON

ILLUSTRATIONS BY JODY BALL

Mom and Dad,

Wow, done with book two. It has been a bit of a bumpy ride and I am glad you helped me through it. You have encouraged me and carefully edited my book. Thank you for all your support. I could not have done it without you. God Bless.

# Table of Contents

Pelios
Vangwick
Hightenmore
Molten
Mountain Pass
Saberlin
Dreylon
Srayo
The
Kala
Lake
Forest of
Torin
Forest of
Bane
The Plains
of
Naldor
Mazaron
Mountains
Seviathan
Fortress
Aphenter
Sadron
Helix
Hills
of the
Gorills
Baciran
Desert
The Bay
of
Cunon
Ioga
of the

Amcronos
Dalto
Ice
Wasteland
Lake
Tibern
The
Towns of
Fairfick
The
Crippling
Swamp
Quoto
The
Towers
of
Woe
Balyon
The Dark Mist
The
Bay
of
Desperation
Peninsula
of
Pafong
Nilon
Maistrale
Falls River
Longland River
Eliz
Bikal
Islor
The
Dragon
Caves
Robas
Forest
of the
Unknown

# PROLOGUE

It all started when ranger Lavrin and his comrade Calix had ventured to the city of Saberlin to buy supplies. Discussing the recent changes in the city, Lavrin and Calix noticed many different things. The house of the lord had become three large towers; new guards stood on the walls, and the emblem of the King no longer hung on those walls. The two had learned from an elderly lady that the city had a new leader named Zekern, who had turned from the ways of the King of Light.

The King of Light, whom Lavrin and Calix followed, represented the way of truth and freedom. Natas ruled most of the land of Amcronos and Zekern was one of many lords under him. Together they fought against the spreading influence of the King of Light. The King taught peace, hope and a better life; Natas, on the other hand, used deceit and trickery along with power and might to keep his lands in check. Long ago, Natas had once stood alongside the King as his chief overseer and advisor, in a land far off the western shores of Amcronos called the Haven Realm. However, Natas had been banished from the side of the King, since he had rebelled against his ways.

Farther into Saberlin, Lavrin and Calix had spied a suspicious person carrying a manuscript out of a building while most of the guards were occupied by an uprising that had erupted near the gate. When they followed the person out of the city and into the forest, they were captured by his comrades. Surprisingly, they discovered that their captors followed the same cause as they did. Learning this, Lavrin and Calix decided to join with them. The three men who had captured Lavrin and Calix took them into their tree house. That night as they all were fast asleep, Lavrin was abruptly awakened by a member of the team who had arrived during the night and had not known he was a friend. She had believed him to be an enemy whom she had fought earlier in her life. She attacked Lavrin viciously and had almost killed him when Chan, their leader, stopped her. Her name was Nadrian, and she was an expert archer. The other two men were Grax, a tall and strong warrior who used axes and hammers, and Felloni, a quiet knife slinger and talented hunter. Like Calix, Chan preferred to use swords as his weaponry. Lavrin used swords as well.

Since Saberlin was neither favorable nor safe, after Lavrin recovered, the group of six had decided to travel to a small town called Dreylon in order to find work and get supplies. The group split and worked in different areas of the small town. After a few days, Calix remembered he had heard of an enemy force moving toward Saberlin from the east. Fighting this band of mercenaries turned out to be more than their small squad could handle. Lavrin was captured and taken to Saberlin, while the rest of the group headed through the forest to try to free him.

Along the way, they met two young children whose house had been burned down. The children were at first cautious, but told them they were headed for a refugee camp to the west. The team decided to escort them there and keep them protected.

Meanwhile in Saberlin's prison, Lavrin met a maiden named Kyra who had been living there for a long while. She had been imprisoned because she had disobeyed her master, Zekern. As the two shared their stories, Lavrin told Kyra about the King he served. She accepted the ways of the King and vowed to follow him.

Soon after, Lavrin heroically battled in the Saberlin arena where he triumphed over his adversary. When he won, he was rewarded with a choice of his freedom or Kyra's. He decided to free Kyra. By Lavrin's instruction, Kyra then fled into the nearby forest and encountered the other members of Lavrin's team.

The rest of the crew, along with Kyra and the children, met a leopard who served the King. He knew that since Saberlin was strongly guarded, they must get help to free Lavrin from Hightenmore. Hightenmore was a castle loyal to the King and was the best place to offer aid. Macrollo also had a special message to deliver to the Lord of Hightenmore, Lord Auden. Before trekking to the castle, they ventured to the refugee camp where they were treated as heroes for returning the lost children. After the warm welcome, they left their kind hosts to continue on toward Hightenmore.

Macrollo, the leopard warrior, was killed on the journey during a fight with enemy hunters. Chan took the message from him to deliver to Lord Auden. Upon arriving at Hightenmore, they told the Lord of Hightenmore of their trials. Meanwhile in Saberlin, an army was being raised by Zekern to attack Hightenmore, in order to weaken the lands of the King of Light in Amcronos.

Upon arriving at the castle, they gave the message to Auden and he greeted them warmly. This letter told them that Hightenmore was in danger from Saberlin to the south. Auden sent spies into Saberlin, and although most were caught, two escaped with valuable information on the enemy's whereabouts. Auden asked Calix and the rest to join his army, which they agreed to do. Kyra felt more qualified as a doctor, while the others became soldiers. As they were knighted, they were given special gifts. Lord Auden also dispatched a force to secretly free Lavrin.

Lord Auden prepared for the oncoming attack, and soon Hightenmore was besieged. The fight was valiant and both sides fought with zeal. Nearing defeat, Hightenmore was miraculously defended from the army of Saberlin through the help of a glorious angel of the King. Many died from the fierce battle, including the loyal Calix.

When victory was accomplished, Lavrin, having been rescued from Saberlin, was reunited with his team in Hightenmore. They were then given an opportunity to venture out of Amcronos and into the Haven Realm. It was a place of peace, perfection and no pain. Most of the small force chose to accept this offer, except for Lavrin, Kyra and Felloni. Bonded in friendship, the three set out to continue their service in Amcronos. For the honor of the King of Light, they would fight the evil power of Natas and spread the King's ways throughout the land.

# CHAPTER 1

# REBUILDING

The sun glittered through a slightly cloudy blue sky. The castle of Hightenmore stood over the Avrick Valley, which separated the castle from nearby forests. It was often noted that Hightenmore looked like the jewel atop a crown from the hill upon which it sat.

Inside the city, people worked to rebuild from the recent battle which had been narrowly won. Since many of the men had been killed during the siege, the women and children stepped up and helped carry the workload. The burial process had recently been completed, with many tears and saddened hearts. Each stone above each buried body was engraved by a relative or friend. Black had been worn throughout the castle as a sign of mourning, while the memory of the brutal battle replayed in every mind. Many lives had been lost in the effort to defend Hightenmore. Only seventy men had survived, forty of whom had been in the battle. One hundred fifty women and one hundred children had survived, many of whom were now father-less or brother-less.

The survivors had tried to forget the siege by repairing Hightenmore. Boards were moved, bricks were hauled and everyone worked to restore the castle to its former glory. The work was hard, but slowly, the castle was in the process of being rebuilt and replenished.

Because the determined people labored constantly, within three weeks they had built fifteen new houses and the blacksmith's shop within the walls. There was still much work to be done, though. The walls were filled with gaps, the stables were gone, and no effort had been attempted yet to remake the villages in the Avrick Valley which surrounded the castle. Young but strong Lavrin, at the age of seventeen, was one of the workers. He diligently helped by carrying supplies and assisting with the reconstruction of the houses.

The city of Hightenmore was a key stronghold for the King's cause. Banners of the King's emblem, a shining sun with a sword striking down in front of it, were displayed throughout Hightenmore.

Lavrin was passionate for the truth of the King of Light and had already fought and been imprisoned for his beliefs. Yet the Lord of Hightenmore, Lord Auden, had sent men secretly into Saberlin who had freed him from his misery.

Lavrin now strolled through the gates and walked the streets of Hightenmore, carrying lumber which had been harvested from the outlining forest. Stone would have been preferred to build the houses, but was in short supply due to repairing the walls. Dropping off the lumber which he was carrying to a group of builders, Lavrin remarked, “Fine work there.”

They smiled faintly. “Thank you, Lavrin.”

After several more hours of work carrying lumber from outside the castle, Lavrin strolled toward the inner castle, surveying his surroundings. He spied boards moving to and fro, hammers pounding nails and some women placing the roofs. He then noticed a man struggling to lift a large rock toward the wall. Lavrin headed toward him to help.

After offering his assistance, Lavrin met with his two comrades, Felloni and Kyra, in the hall of the main castle. Felloni was a silent and shy character who was an expert hunter and knife master. He had short brown hair and a thin frame. Kyra was not of the fighting type, but rather served as an apprentice doctor. She had long red hair which she often braided, and was caring and kind to not only her patients but also to everyone she met. She was temporarily in training with two other doctors in the army.

The three of them gazed upon a display which held the swords of their comrades. Each sword had a special handle formed in the shape of an animal’s head, each animal representing the person who carried it. After the battle, their friends had left Amcronos and had journeyed to the land of the King across the sea, the Haven Realm. The Haven Realm was a land of mystery foretold to be a place of wonder and brilliance, where pain was but a memory. The three were all that was left of the Knights of Torin. They had decided to stay in Amcronos, believing that the King still had tasks for them.

As it was getting late, the trio decided to walk toward the campfire where they would be eating along with the rest of the soldiers and townsfolk. Upon arriving at the campfire, they saw all the people talking and eating. The cook gave each of them a platter of food, including venison, berries and a slice of oat bread. One of the soldiers tried to lighten the mood by singing a merry tune, and others began to sing along. One boy began to play the fiddle while another played the flute. Soon all the people were dancing. This was an encouraging sign that the people were temporarily forgetting their hardships and the losses they had suffered.

Lavrin stood up and asked Kyra, “May I have this dance?”

She laughed, “Why, certainly.”

Lavrin and Kyra swayed joyously around the fire. Everyone danced and circled the flickering flames, singing the merry tune. Everyone except for Felloni, who sat slowly eating and watching the flames of the fire leap as if in a trance. He did not even seem to notice the singing or laughter or dancing. To him, the dance of the fire far surpassed the dance of the others.

The song soon died down and everyone relaxed with food and drink around the fire again. They all chatted and chuckled until Lord Auden was seen leaving the castle, walking in their direction and holding a book in his hand.

When he arrived at the scene with the large purple and gold book, he called for everyone's attention. "Dear citizens and soldiers of Hightenmore, I have been reading from a book called *The King's Histories* and would like to read everyone a poem written by a lord many years ago. In this poem, he showed that although he faced troubling times, he stayed true to the King."

Auden began reading:

"The King is my shepherd; little shall I desire. He lays me in meadows and grants me water. He restores me and guides me down pure paths for the glory of his name. Though I am tempted and wounded I will never give up because he will heal me. He prepares me in my enemies' midst, and anoints me so abundantly that my blessings overflow. Surely goodness, peacefulness and charity shall be with me always. Someday I will dwell in the place of my King's light forever."

Lavrin lifted up his cup to offer a toast. "To the glory and truth of the King."

Everyone cheered, "To the glory and truth of the King."

The meal was soon finished and everyone headed to their place of lodging. Some traveled to the newly built houses, others slept in the castle, and a few were content sleeping outside. Lavrin, Kyra and Felloni offered the more comfortable lodging to others and slept under the stars.

The three lay in the tall grass and gazed upon the dazzling stars which blanketed the dark night sky. Each unique, together they sparkled in graceful unison. Amidst the shimmering constellations, the moon shone brightest of all. Sleepiness soon drifted through the trees outside the castle like a thief creeping in the night, and the three closed their tired eyes to prepare for another day.

Early the next morning, Felloni splashed a bucket of cold water onto Lavrin, instantly jolting him awake. Smirking, Felloni remarked, "You promised you would wake up early today to train." After drying himself, Lavrin followed Felloni to a small plot of ground where they trained. Felloni slung knives masterfully while rolling to the side in the dirt, three of the four knives hitting the centers of the targets. Lavrin trained with two other soldiers, teaching them techniques of stabbing, parrying and finding an opponent's weakness. They quickly learned that they needed to work off each other's strengths to counter Lavrin's strong yet precise strokes.

All the while, Kyra sat nearby, watching them and reading her medical book. The book she had been given shared the effects of different ailments and which herbs to be used on them. By the end of the previous battle, Kyra had healed many a wound and helped save quite a few lives. Yet she was far from finished with her studies.

The clash of weapons was mixed with the bashing sounds of the tools in the background. Lord Auden walked amongst the workers, delegating tasks. Some people brought stones, others cut them, while still others lifted them into place and filled in the gaps of the walls with mortar. The inner wall was partially completed and once again looked strong, but the outer wall remained in disrepair.

Suddenly a lone horseman wearing the King's emblem on his chest bolted into the city, trampling on the dirt road and heading straight toward the main castle. This confused many of the townsfolk, and they pondered, "Why has an unexpected rider entered town?" Rumors were suggested but nothing was certain.

Felloni and Lavrin decided to continue their training with a duel to teach the others their techniques. Since they had worked several days in the rebuilding effort, the new recruits had been assigned a day's break. Lavrin said, "The great King of Light, may he live and reign forever, and may his followers prosper." This saying was quoted often, because it was the King's motto.

Felloni replied, "Agreed."

In front of the soldiers in training, Lavrin asked, "So my friend of few words, shall we begin the duel?"

He nodded. Lavrin drew a wooden sword while Felloni drew two wooden knives. Kyra closed her book and watched the two soldiers prepare to duel one another. She knew that although they were dueling with wood, it was going to be a very serious match.

Felloni charged at Lavrin, and rolled under his sword stab but Lavrin spun away as he tried to stab him in the back. Lavrin swung for his legs but Felloni jumped over it. Felloni knocked Lavrin's sword out of his hands but Lavrin placed a kick in Felloni's chest, sending him backward.

Lavrin leaned back and picked up his sword while dodging a knife thrown just above his head. Felloni quickly drew another knife while Lavrin regained his balance. This knife was blocked, but Lavrin and Felloni were soon at each other's throats. Rolling across the ground, they each tried to get an edge over the other. The wrestling continued until they broke apart. Lavrin grabbed one of Felloni's knives. Felloni grabbed the other knife, and they each threw them, hitting the other at the same time. As both got up, Kyra clapped from the side. They shook hands and began to wipe the sweat from their faces with cloths. Kyra yelled out, "Good fight." Lavrin bowed.

Suddenly a guard rushed down from the wall; a look of surprise covered his face. "An army comes from the city of Vanswick!"

Everyone quickly rushed past the outer wall to see a large group of soldiers, well-armed and with armor reflecting the light of the sun. Lord Auden was the first to greet the army led by a friend of his, Lord Denethor. Lord Denethor was the elder of the two, but still had as much zeal as Auden. Denethor's hair was gray and he was of average height, but he was known to be extremely passionate and loyal. The army seemed to number around six to seven hundred troops, but the people of Hightenmore were both too glad to see their old friends of Vanswick and too shocked at their arrival to count.

Lord Auden embraced Lord Denethor and questioned, "I received your messenger who told me you would be arriving, yet why the sense of urgency?"

Lord Denethor announced, "I have heard of the valiant struggle which your men so faithfully endured from your previous letter. Now I believe the time has come for action, and I have rallied my forces."

Lord Auden remarked, "You can see that the castle is still under repair. Nevertheless, let us discuss this action you have in mind in the main hall."

Lord Auden, Lord Denethor, Lavrin, Kyra and Felloni headed for the hall with the other advisors of both lords, while the warriors of Vanswick got the best welcome the survivors could muster. Lavrin and his two friends were allowed to participate in the discussion because they were three of the people most trusted by Auden.

In the hall, the lords, consultants and comrades made their way to a special round table in the back of the hall. The table had a large detailed map of all the surrounding territory, from the Forest of Bane to the city of Srayo.

The ten sat down and Lord Denethor began to express what he thought was the best course of action. "After your victory, I rallied my troops from Vanswick and the surrounding countryside, and came here as soon as possible. The time has come. We must move soon to seize this opportunity. Saberlin's guard numbers little to none, because we both know that he sent everything he had against Hightenmore. Yet what I know, but you may not, is that a fourth of his troops were from the city of Srayo to the east. I believe we can reach Saberlin before any more significant amount of reinforcements can arrive from Srayo.

"Also, since Saberlin is the main gateway into the Northwest, and Srayo is practically the only place that can send it reinforcements, now is the time to fight. If we can secure Saberlin, Srayo will then probably be unprepared, thinking that once we secured Saberlin we would want to regroup. That is just what we want. The element of surprise would give us an advantage over Srayo. If we used this and captured Srayo, we could not only control the Northwest, but also the mountain pass and all Northwestern trade.

"I believe this is the King's sign to us that he is opening the door to a secure, strong, safe and solid platform which he can use to spread his good name. I have already shared this with my forces, and together we have my six hundred thirty and your forty which make an army of six hundred seventy soldiers. All trained and all loyal."

Lord Auden stared at the map, going over Lord Denethor's plan in his mind. He looked up. "It might work. It is very sudden, but it could work. What are your views, Lavrin?"

He replied, "I believe it may work, and I see the logic. Yet I can't help but wonder who will manage Hightenmore and Vanswick while the rest of us are on this crusade? As you know, Hightenmore is still under repair and reconstruction from the last attack."

Lord Denethor answered rapidly, almost anticipating that this question would be asked. "I have set my wife in charge of Vanswick; she is smart and resourceful. I have given her a lot of advice with which to govern Vanswick."

Lord Auden spoke. "I would set you three as managers of Hightenmore, but you will be needed in the battles. I will set my overseer who has been helping to guide the work in

Hightenmore in charge. Although he is slightly impatient, he is a good leader."

After a few other matters were discussed and the plan was edited, Kyra asked, "When shall we set out?"

Lord Denethor replied, "As quickly as possible. With each hour that passes the opening slowly closes."

The group moved outside and proceeded to direct the preparation of the troops to begin the journey. Since the weary army of Vanswick was tired and it was getting late, everyone rested to gain their strength.

As the morning sun climbed up the horizon, the men were awakened. Within several hours everything was set, partially because the Vanswick troops came ready to leave. Food was gathered, and weapons were distributed. Siege weapons which had been repaired after the battle were carried by the men. Soon the army, six hundred seventy strong, marched through the outer gate and soon disappeared into the forest, ready to face any foe in their path, especially the guards of Saberlin.

# CHAPTER 2

# THE EXPEDITION

Lavrin pushed a branch away from his face as the group treaded through thick shrubbery and trees. Sadly, most of the fighters had to walk on foot. Horses were limited since most of them were only found farther to the south. Felloni, though, felt right at home in the forest. He loved smelling the clean air and drinking the stream water. The shadows of the trees overlapped the rays of sunshine, and the chirping song of birds was ever-present.

Felloni had ventured moderately far in front of the group to scout and hunt. He had rubbed mud on his face and arms and wore a leather suit as camouflage. Suddenly, he noticed a wild turkey rummaging around the undergrowth. The hunt was on. Felloni leaped over a berry bush like a lion chasing down a gazelle. The turkey squealed and squabbled as it tried to outmaneuver Felloni and reach safety, but Felloni was not easily outwitted.

Felloni dove and grabbed the turkey by the legs. It scrambled in protest but Felloni held firm. Soon the turkey was finished and Felloni smiled at his first catch of the day. When Felloni returned to the army, he gave Lord Auden the turkey and told him the clearest route for the army to continue.

Auden remarked, "You should be focusing on your task ahead, not hunting."

Felloni shrugged, "Hunting and scouting are my passion."

A young soldier walked up to Felloni and asked him, "Are you Felloni, one of the leaders in the defense of Hightenmore?" Felloni nodded.

The soldier continued, "Did you really see the mighty angel of the King?"

Felloni replied, "He was quite a sight to behold. He wore a long robe, his body glowed like many stars and the blade of his sword was pure fire." The soldier's eyes widened and he went off to tell the other soldiers, since the rumors had spread far and wide of the heroic stand in Hightenmore.

Meanwhile, Lavrin and Lord Denethor walked side by side with Kyra close behind them. Lavrin's litz had formed a strong bond with Kyra and lay asleep in her pouch. Oddly, it slept soundly, even with the supplies and the medical book jostling around in the bag also.

Lavrin asked Lord Denethor, "What is the city of Vanswick like?"

He smiled. "I have led Vanswick for many years and have grown to know its people as family. Vanswick is an honorable city known for the rivers which flow near its walls. Vanswick's people are always prepared to give to those in need and have never rebelled, even in tough times. Sometimes people will come and watch our soldiers train to support them. If you walk through the streets, you will find many people talking and laughing while they go about their work. As for me, I have a wife and three daughters, and live in a mansion at the north part of Vanswick. I try to hear the needs of the people and take them into consideration, yet I keep taxes low, so there are usually few troubles."

Lavrin said, "That sounds like a remarkable place to live." Abruptly, Lavrin tripped on a long root and landed on the ground with a thud. Kyra helped him up, giggling, "You might want to keep your eyes on the path, soldier."

The army continued to make steady progress, and had a constant supply of food from the forest wildlife.

*****

In the city of Saberlin, past the rich treasures stolen by Zekern's thugs, Zekern was trying to shrug off the nagging disappointment and stress over the loss at Hightenmore castle. Zekern slumped in his throne with his robe outlined in silver pulled tight around him. Although only a lord, he wanted to feel like an emperor. These pleasures which he surrounded himself with greatly taxed the townsfolk, yet he did not care.

On the table in front of him lay two roasted pigs, three platters of grapes, four pies, each of a different type and flavor, and five selections of wine. Upon a decorative tablecloth, the food looked like the feast for many kings. To his left sat his favorite wife. She wore a long blue dress with a silver necklace around her neck, and a silver crown resting on her head. To his right sat his top advisor. He was a stout man with a short, curly mustache, whose face displayed his arrogance and pride.

Zekern took three slices of pork, one bunch of grapes, a slice of meat pie and a cup full of wine. Although it was scrumptious, Zekern barely ate the meal, and called for entertainment to be brought to distract him from his troubles. The castle of Hightenmore had been his ultimate desire, and it had been snatched away from him right before he could acquire it.

First the jester, dressed in a suit of red, blue and yellow, approached the lord. The jester took out five colored juggling balls which matched his outfit and began wildly tossing them behind his back and through his legs. His crazy stunts occupied the lord only for fifteen minutes, and the jester was sent away.

Next came Zekern's scribe, who read the lord accounts of his triumphs. This pleased him mildly, but what he really wanted was the shining castle of Hightenmore, overlooking the Avrick Valley, as his greatest prize. Hightenmore was not only a stronghold for the Light; it also possessed many trade routes and loyal subjects.

Zekern left the feast. He had decided that, to satisfy his vengeance, there would be a tournament at the arena where prisoners would fight one another as well as various beasts.

Within a couple of hours, around midday, Zekern was seated above the arena in a booth made especially for him and his prized wife. The stands slowly began to fill with people, ready for a fight. The skirmishes soon began. The fight which probably interested the lord the most was a fight in which two warriors faced a lion. Each fighter was given a spear and a shield, plus limited armor. The fight was fierce, but in the end the lion killed both of the prisoners. The crowd roared from the stands.

After the fight had ended, one of Zekern's spies rushed into the lord's booth. Zekern turned and spat, "You are not allowed to be in here."

Panting for breath, he whispered, "Lord, I have important news. An army has been spotted to the north over six hundred strong, coming from the direction of Hightenmore. They are a few days away. We need to set up defenses before they arrive."

Zekern was immediately out of his chair, bolting past the man and pushing him aside. Thoughts raced through his head. "How did they get an army so fast? Then another thought entered his mind. Vanswick could have given reinforcements. Another question. Did they have an army of six hundred strong this whole time, waiting until he was weak?"

Zekern knew there was little time to debate with himself now. Time was walking away. Zekern rocketed toward the stable. He gathered two of his best messengers; each mounted the fastest horse available and sped toward Srayo. Zekern assembled his guard of about ninety. The city of Saberlin was placed on alert. All the guards rushed about - some got weaponry, and others closed and blockaded the gate.

Two days passed and Zekern had done everything possible to make Saberlin defendable. On the third day, seventy troops arrived from Srayo, along with his two messengers.

When they reached Saberlin, Zekern saw the small band and was confused as to why only seventy arrived when he had expected two hundred or more. One of the messengers leading the band delivered a message to Zekern, which stated:

**Dear Lord Zekern,**

**I assume you see that I have only sent a small number of troops to your aid. This is due to the fact that I have limited troops to spare, after you lost them all at the siege of Hightenmore. At the moment, I need to focus more on the needs of Srayo than on your needs. I hope you will succeed this time at defending Saberlin because Natas will not be amused otherwise.**

**The Lord of Srayo**

Zekern read the letter and spat on the dirt. He would prove that he was still worthy of his title, and that he could defend Saberlin with one hundred sixty against six hundred or more. Somehow he would show his usefulness to Natas in both battle and leadership… somehow.

# CHAPTER 3

# CONFRONTATION

Light embraced both of the armies. The sun was shining brightly, and a cool breeze swept the faces of the warriors. Each side had strategies to defeat the other. Lord Auden had made the troops bring grappling hooks and siege ladders to scale the walls. Zekern, on the other hand, had prepared cauldrons of boiling oil to be poured upon the enemy. He also had archers lined up, all along the western wall. Lord Auden and Lord Denethor knew that they would have to find a way to limit the influence of the enemy archers. They both decided that when the troops charged with the scaling mechanisms, they would hold up their shields, using the light in their favor.

Between the forces lay the grassy meadows that surrounded Saberlin. These plains were filled with blossoming flowers of all varieties and butterflies adorned with beautiful patterns across their wings. Thin grass stood tall and covered the area. Soon the toll of war would stomp on this place as well.

Lavrin told Kyra, "You will need to stay behind, because it will be far too dangerous for you to scale the enemy walls."

She opened her mouth to protest, but Lavrin placed his finger over it, and stared into her passionate eyes. "Please, Kyra, trust me. You need to stay behind." She understood and remained at the makeshift camp; besides, she would need to prepare the medical tents for the wounded.

It was also decided that Lavrin and Felloni would lead this mission with the commanders. While the battle occurred, the lords would strategize their next actions and direct from the camp.

Felloni twirled his knife in his hand as he often did when perplexed or in deep thought. This battle would be harsh but crucial to the Forces of Light. The camouflage had been wiped off his face, since it would be of little use now, and his straight, firm features were more visible. Felloni also carried a grappling hook and rope in his other hand which he would use to ascend Saberlin. Lavrin would be carrying a ladder with three other soldiers. Each would raise their shield with one hand and use the other to carry the ladder.

Lavrin called out to the army, loud enough for them all to hear, but quiet enough for the defenders not to, because they were half a mile away. "This day, may we show our valor for the King, for truth and for freedom. May it be said of us that we never gave up and never feared. Lastly, may it be known throughout Amcronos that we reclaimed Saberlin and gave all our effort and all of our power to make sure that no one could stand against us. Yet let us not do this in a way of revenge, frustration or spite. Let us show mercy if possible, but let us never give up. We will take Saberlin this day for the glory of the King!"

The attackers cheered from the heroic speech. Replaying both the plan of attack and the message in their hearts, the troop readied their courage and morale for the siege. Slowly, they drew their weapons and readied their long shields, and at once they charged forth past the oak and pine trees and across the open plain.

The archers on top of Saberlin's walls fired down arrows; some found their targets, but most were off due to the reflected light or only found their way into sturdy metal shields. As the soldiers of Light began to ascend, boiling oil flung many off the ladders and onto the ground in pain. Lavrin climbed up the ladder swiftly. He jumped upon the wall just as an enemy pushed the ladder off. Lavrin managed to grab it and pull it back up to the wall while dodging a thrust meant for his chest. His sword was jabbed into the chest of the opponent in retaliation, and the defender of Saberlin was soon motionless.

Felloni had easily ascended the wall with precision as Lavrin had, and was now engaged with a tall, strong warrior wearing thick armor and armed with a long sword which he held in both hands.

The rest of the soldiers of Light who had successfully avoided the arrows and oil and had not been pushed from their ladders were atop the wall. The intense brawl between the sides left it difficult to tell who was on which side. Arrows zoomed and the impact of metal on metal created powerful noise.

Bodies fell, weapons collided, and screams of pain were mixed with yells of rage. At some points during the siege, it looked as if the defenders of Saberlin had the upper hand, but then, banding together, those of the Light cut into their opponents' weaknesses and returned the favor.

Lavrin barely blocked a mace directed toward a wounded soldier and then rolled past a downward sword. He ducked under a high swing then completed a left up-striking combination.

Suddenly, his focus shifted. Where was that slippery cod? Then he saw him - Zekern, dressed in black armor outlined in red, with a long two-handed sword whose blade was sharp on both sides and was like his armor, black outlined in red. His helmet was large and had numerous black spikes extending from it. Zekern was especially tall, and his eyes glared with anger and determination. Lavrin had finally earned his chance to pay back the punishment which Zekern had put him through.

Zekern's troops soon retreated off the wall to the courtyard in a triangle formation, at which Zekern was the forward point. Zekern's sword was constantly in motion, cutting down the King's troops. Lavrin was met by an axe wielder. Lavrin blocked an axe thrust with his shield, kicked the assailant in the stomach and finished him. He then spun to the side, ducked under an arrow and hit a soldier's legs with his sword.

Felloni grabbed an opponent's spear as it was thrown at him and stabbed it into an enemy charging from behind. He then was knocked off by a hammer, but managed to launch a knife at the spear thrower, hitting him in the leg. The man reeled back in pain and Felloni, back on his feet, side-kicked the small, crafty hammer-wielding soldier, sending him to the ground.

He then quickly flipped out a knife which he used to block an enemy's sword. Felloni spin-kicked the combatant across the face, and knocked him to the ground.

Zekern ragingly attacked the foes in front of him. One unlucky man was grabbed at the throat. The man was plummeted to the ground, his life ended by a sword through the heart. Zekern then spun with sword outstretched in a full circle, wounding a few.

Lavrin was having less luck. He directed his blade to deflect a sudden mace attack. Although it was mostly deflected, the spikes sliced across Lavrin's hand, causing him to lose his grip on his sword. He had lost his sword and now had to resort to his shield and fist fighting. Lavrin elbowed a foe but received a hammer to the shoulder from a second fighter whom he had not seen to his left.

Lavrin jumped up from the dirt and now realized that three adversaries had cornered him up against the wall. One, with scars running across his grimacing face and tough arms, held a long double-sided axe. The second, of average height, had a pointed nose and wore armor which was coated with fresh blood along the side. He was armed with two spears. The third held a large hammer that had spikes on the ends and also carried a thin short sword. He had a round face which wore an angry grimace as well. Lavrin knew his only chance was to get a weapon before they could all attack him.

Lavrin sprang into action with cheetah-like reflexes. He slammed his shield to the left, chopped one opponent's wrist, grabbed his axe and barely escaped by diving through the same opponent's legs. With axe in hand, he landed two precise movements to wound two of the three. Unexpectedly, this left him vulnerable to the third man's spear, which slammed into Lavrin's side. Lavrin struggled to overcome the pain, but drew the spear out of his flesh and continued the fight.

While the battle unfolded, Kyra sat staring at the castle, hoping her comrades were safe. She held her face in her hands, wishing desperately she could do something to help. All she could do now was hope and listen to the fierce sounds erupting inside the broad stone wall surrounding Saberlin. Suddenly, a man leading a group of wounded combatants called to her. Kyra then focused on treating the injured soldiers who had been dragged from the plains and had just arrived at the medical tents.

Kyra tried to interpret the news of the horrific battle from the messengers informing the lords, but it only left her confused and stressed, so she focused on her patients. Lord Auden paced eagerly yet nervously, also desperate for more news of the crucial siege. Lord Denethor sat on the uncomfortable earth, staring blankly at a long parchment containing a map of the Northwest, much like that seen at Hightenmore, but larger. Also he had a map of the castle of Srayo which was intricately detailed. Denethor looked for gaps in the defense system yet could not find any. He considered a rear attack but they would be spotted. Calculating battle strategies was often difficult, but Denethor knew it was crucial.

Inside Saberlin, bodies fell from both sides. Lavrin made sure that as many of the few remaining guards of Saberlin that could be spared were spared. Zekern found himself with ten guards left. The number soon dropped to five. Lavrin, Felloni and the remainder of the army surrounded the six. The fight was now of little contest. Zekern was surrounded and bound, then thrown with ten others into the prison. Lavrin personally made sure that Zekern was placed in the same cell that he and Kyra had been kept in. That way, he would endure the same pain he had felt.

The gates were opened to Saberlin, and Felloni loudly trumpeted the horn to alert the others at camp that victory was accomplished. Kyra and the lords hurried upon the city. It was a brutal scene, to say the least. Friend and foe lay together across the cobblestone streets, soon to share nearby earthen graves. Although few houses had faced serious damage, it looked as if the whole city had been attacked.

When those from camp arrived, Kyra rushed up to Lavrin and helped him stumble into one of the medical tents, battered on the shoulder, bleeding on the hand and desperately weak and tired. He also had been wounded by the spear inflicted in his side. Sweat ran off his face and his hair. She brought him to a bed just as he collapsed.

A few hours later, Kyra told him, "I thought you might not make it. Thankfully, most of your injuries were nonfatal and you will recover soon."

Lavrin replied weakly, “I guess I’m a man of surprises.”

Kyra then got to work with the few other doctors to aid the wounded still living.

Felloni knelt over the body of a dead soldier. He looked at the combatant’s face and recognized the young man who had so curiously questioned him about the victory at Hightenmore. Felloni rose. He knew nothing could be done for the lad, but hoped that his soul had made its way to the Haven Realm far across the sea. It was a strange phenomenon caused by the King. His followers who died did not really die; their spirits went to the Haven Realm to live anew.

Meanwhile, Kyra and the other doctors were rapidly demanding able-bodied soldiers to move wounded soldiers. As Kyra wrapped a severed leg with a bandage, the other doctors were treating an unfortunate arrow victim. Soldiers were continually carried in and laid on long white stretchers, soon to be white no longer – some soldiers with cuts and deep bruises while others with more serious ailments. Help was supplied as much as possible from the other soldiers, but most of the burden was on the doctors.

*****

The next day, the King’s emblem was once more displayed all across the city of Saberlin. Civilians cheered their new heroes, glad to be released of their greedy, tyrannical ruler. The soldiers lifted up a song of reverence to the King in one voice:

“The King! The King! The glorious King of Light!

For him! For him! We always will fight.

His ways. His ways. Forever will stay pure.

For him. For him. We'll constantly endure."

All the townsfolk of Saberlin hung white cloths over their doors to symbolize the new hope they had in a better life under the King. The lords headed toward Zekern's cell, eager to learn any information possible which might aid them in attacking Srayo. While they walked, they discussed the details of how they would get information from Zekern, since he was as stubborn as a turtle refusing to come out of its shell.

Lord Denethor inserted the key into the rusty slot, opened the door and found Zekern sitting on the floor. His hair was messy and his clothes torn, obviously from frustration over his loss in the battle. Zekern had been chained to the wall by both of his arms. Dust filled the air and dirt accumulated across the room's floor and brick walls. The room was mostly dark, except for rays of light which crept in from the barred window. Mold and grime infested the walls, making them utterly filthy.

Zekern lifted up his face and screamed at the two lords, "I will tell you nothing! Nothing! I will kill you all someday, and when I do I won't make it quick. Get out now! I might be chained but you can't make me talk. I will hunt you down when I escape! That or kill me now! Right now!"

The lords stepped outside to reconsider their position, while Zekern continued screaming as if a howler monkey deprived of its food. Lord Auden led Lord Denethor outside the prison after relocking the door. "I don't believe the time is right to interrogate him," said Lord Auden.

Denethor replied, "Certainly, he will be a handful."

The lords split, each to attend other matters in the city. Thankfully they did not need to deal with the citizens, because most were happy for the change in leadership, especially after hearing of how the dwellers of Hightenmore and Vanswick fared.

*****

Lavrin watched his litz and his dog Vin chase one another across the plains just outside Saberlin. A litz is a small scaly dragon, slightly larger than most songbirds, often used as a messenger. Each litz has a gem on its back and because of this, the litz species had become increasingly rare. People often would kill litz to get their gems and sell them in markets or to rich landowners. Vin and the litz seemed to be locked in a game of "bite the competitor in the tail." Vin, of course, was at a large disadvantage since the litz could fly.

Lavrin remembered the times when Calix, his longest and dearest friend, would hide in the forest, and Vin would scavenge until he found him. It took Vin almost an hour to find Calix once. Calix had hidden on top of the roof of their tree house, a place Vin would never expect. Skinning a recent catch, Lavrin urged Vin on, saying, "Where is he, Vin?" and "Find Calix, Vin." Eventually Vin began to howl. He had found his prey. Calix descended from the roof and stroked the small terrier.

Lavrin watched the two creatures play. Calix now lived in a different place. He had died in the battle of Hightenmore and now lived in the presence of the King. After the fateful battle, their group had been given the opportunity to escape death and be transported to the Haven Realm for their valiant deeds. Most of the small band chose the King's land, but Lavrin, Felloni and Kyra decided to continue their service in Amcronos.

*****

Felloni was also thinking. He was inside the room in which Zekern stored his treasures. There was one tall cushioned chair in the room on which Felloni sat. The room had a large window to the left, and displays of tapestry and riches to the right. Some of the riches had been recently added by Zekern's obsession with money and power. Others were heirlooms of the lords before him. There were gems, swords, vases and maps on long silk tablecloths stretched over mahogany tables.

Felloni compared the scenic view with the riches. Each had a unique beauty which the other did not. Felloni thought about the similarities and differences between them. Out the window, overlooking the city's broad stone walls, a red and purple sunset cast its light on the numerous trees and the grassy plains which surrounded Saberlin. Majestic birds flew in the sky. Felloni saw a river flowing through the trees, its waters rushing rapidly. He gazed as the trees swayed in the wind.

The riches, on the other hand, showed power and honor - symbols of human skill and accomplishment. Tassels hung from the tapestry and each golden, silver or bronze item was decoratively engraved with various patterns. Each possession was perfectly polished and seemed to show the arrogant yet masterful ways of man. Smells of rich spices drifted through the air.

Both scenes were desirable in their own way. Each left impressions on a man or woman's thoughts, such as the feelings of greed, awe, or curiosity.

# CHAPTER 4

# ACQUIRED KNOWLEDGE

The new day rose with speed and the city had already begun to function. All of the soldiers had risen at sunrise to bury those who had deceased. It seemed that the burial grounds of both Hightenmore and Saberlin had doubled in size. This was a sad but understandable truth. One of the pleasant things was that most of the buildings which had been "bruised" were easily fixed. The army slept in the barracks and the inhabitants continued most of their regular routines in the usual manner but with cheerful spirits.

Kyra felt droplets of rain splash down lightly. Usually people thought that rain was a sign of sorrow, but not Kyra; she thought changes in weather were just that - weather. Kyra walked over to Felloni who had just finished digging the burial holes with several other men. She pondered, “It seems like we won too easily. Would you agree?”

Felloni nodded. Kyra then asked, “Are you thinking again, or in a bad mood?”

Felloni continued to dig with his shovel and whispered barely loud enough for Kyra to hear, “A bit of both.” Kyra quizzically watched him work, then directed her steps toward the barracks to check on her recovering patients.

She was happy to find that most of the wounded were recovering steadily and she tended to those who needed attention. One soldier had been diagnosed with fever, which had probably started on the journey to Saberlin. She swabbed his forehead with a wet rag, trying to calm the sickness. The man smiled as much as he could muster.

Soon a guard yelled out from a watchtower atop the southern wall, “A group comes from the south. They number around fifty.” The lords and Lavrin, who had been thoroughly discussing the plan of attack on Srayo, ran toward the gate, utterly confused. What would anyone from the south come north for? Did they know Saberlin had been liberated?

The guard yelled to them, “Friend or foe?”

They all yelled, “Friend, Friend. We follow the King and rejoice to see his emblem on the walls of Saberlin once again.”

When the fifty or so entered, they looked worn, hungry and ragged. They wore torn clothing and looked sad and tired. Immediately, food was brought to them. One of the women began to inform the lords of the situation. "The refugee camp to the south has been invaded." She took a few deep breaths. "Most of the refugees were killed; we fled here to try to escape and beg for help."

Lavrin asked, "Who attacked the camp?"

A young boy answered, "Scary lizards that stood on two feet and carried sharp weapons. They yelled really loud."

Everyone looked at one another with confused and questioning expressions. Another woman from the camp told them, "It's true, creatures from the mountains. They had scaly skin and were beasts of outstanding rage and slaughter."

One man from Saberlin called out, "Has anyone heard of such a beast?" No one answered for a long while until a loud voice pronounced from behind the crowd. "They are the Seviathans."

All eyes turned to see a giant eagle atop the peak of the castle who was taller than a man. His eyes were deep purple as were the tips of his wings and his beak, but most of his body was a brownish gold. He had two straps which crossed his chest and held a plethora of unique darts.

He flew down right next to the crowd. "They are a race of half-lizard, half-men first discovered by Natas during the time the King's messengers first arrived. They have enslaved the villages of the Mazaron Mountains to the south for decades. The villages are used as a work force for the Seviathans. These creatures have scaly skin and a long tail ending in spikes, yet stand on two feet. They have precise smell and vision, but they yell loudly due to their lacking sense of hearing. They have five fingered hands but three toed feet. The Seviathan language consists of babbles and shrieks which very few who are not Seviathan can understand. Not even me."

Felloni inquired of him, "How do you possess such knowledge?"

He squawked, "I am Idrellon, scribe of the King. Long have I recorded the details of the events and creatures of Amcronos, the Seviathans being one of them. I am glad that Saberlin has returned to the Light as it had when under Paricus, the father of Zekern."

The survivors of the attack were taken to some of the empty houses in Saberlin and given places to quarter. Many of them decided that they wished to dwell in Saberlin permanently. One young boy, who had night-black hair, wore dirty brown trousers and a long sleeved brown shirt, walked up to Idrellon and said, "I am Eli. My friend Macrollo once told me about you."

Idrellon replied, "Yes, Macrollo, the leopard warrior. He was a valiant fighter but now lives in the Haven Realm."

Eli remarked, "My sister said that I would never get to meet you, but now that I have, you are much taller than I expected."

"It is a pleasure to meet you too, my small friend," Idrellon chuckled. Eli smiled and ran off to the place he was staying, a small wooden house with one door and no windows just to the side of the center street.

Lord Auden and Lord Denethor walked into Zekern's study and locked the door behind them. They had discovered the key attached to a chain which Zekern had worn across his neck.

They looked around; numerous books horded the shelves and the two small wooden chairs were placed around a table of marble. A clear window engulfed them in light and the dark stone floor had a glossy appeal. "What do you think, Auden? Is this worth investigating? I mean, I have seen a lot of things, but lizard men? I don't know."

Lord Auden ran his fingers across his chin where his short goatee lay and eventually whispered, "If it is true, it needs to be looked into, but we must take Srayo while the time is right. We must act before Srayo learns of Saberlin's fall and is reinforced."

Lord Denethor paused. "I agree, we can't spare many troops. Then again, if these Seviathans are serious killers as the eagle has described them, we will need the best to fight them."

Lord Auden replied, "Let me send Lavrin, Felloni, Kyra and seventeen other top warriors. That way we won't lose too many men, but the fighters will be experienced enough to attack these beasts if they are as dangerous as mentioned. Since they have killed many of the men in the refugee camp, they must be quite strong. Lavrin and Felloni know the forests and could easily lead the small force to the refugee camp and then up into the mountains."

Lord Denethor pondered, "Will we still be able to take Srayo with the loss of twenty men, who are some of our top soldiers?"

Lord Auden stood up. "That's it! We persuade the eagle, who believes the Seviathans are a threat, that if we were to send twenty men to fight against the Seviathans, we would need his help. With Idrellon on our side, we would be sure to take Srayo."

Lord Denethor walked to the door, unlocked it with the short brass key and, after first holding open the door for Auden, left the cluttered study. Luckily for them, Idrellon had decided to stay until help was brought to the refugee camp, because he knew that the Seviathans were a severe enemy to the Forces of Light and must be dealt with.

The lords now entered the streets in search of their flying friend and spied him cleaning his feathers with his beak near the barracks. The large maple tree beside him covered him in shade. The lords picked up their courage, took a deep breath, and approached Idrellon. He stopped his cleaning and looked up at them. "Is there a problem?"

Lord Denethor answered, "Not quite a problem, more a thought."

Idrellon stated, "I would be glad to advise you and help this situation in any way possible."

Lord Denethor continued, "We have heard the plight of the refugees and have decided to send twenty capable soldiers with a lot of battle experience to investigate. That said, I must ask you to help the remaining army in the taking of Srayo. If we can succeed in this quest, the Northwest region shall be secure for the King."

Idrellon responded, "I myself am not the greatest of the King's creatures in the art of battle. Yet I will fight. I can see that Srayo is key to stabilizing the King's lands. I wish a more skilled warrior could help you, but they are occupied fighting the evil beasts of Natas." The lords bowed and he returned the gesture.

Next was the task of creating the team to head south. They would need to be well armed in case they encountered Seviathans. They must also be well experienced.

Lavrin, Felloni, Kyra and seventeen other combatants stood in a row while being addressed by the lords. "You twenty chosen warriors are to journey down toward the refugee camp to discover any possible Seviathan troops, and if found, to try to eliminate them. If there are too many to defeat, you are to contact us through Lavrin's litz who will be traveling with you. You will be given sufficient weapons and supplies for the expedition. You will set off tomorrow evening."

Idrellon added, "The Seviathans rely on their smell, so masking yours will be important. Travel swiftly while in the mountains and try to stay off the center paths because that is where they will likely be found. If encountered, flee only when necessary as they will react strongly to signs of weakness. Remember to avoid any large groups of Seviathans and help any survivors found at the refugee camp if there are any. Are there any questions?"

No one responded, so they headed off to pack their supplies. Weapons would be provided tomorrow. Kyra carefully packed all of her medical items into a leather bag which strapped around her shoulder. Most of them packed personal belongings and blankets while some began to pack food and water.

When the team was awakened the next morning, everyone set to work on final preparations. The twenty visited the armory where they received new weapons. It was a stone building with a tall chimney on the right wall. The door was thin and made of a light brown wood. Above it hung a sign with two hammers crossed, symbolizing a blacksmith. Inside, a warm heat emitted from the intense fire in the stove. The low ceiling was uncomfortable for some. There was a rack on every side organized neatly by weapon class. One rack was of axes, two of swords, one of bows and another of special type.

A strong man walked out from a back room with his arms filled to the brim with weapons. He called, "Gather around! Here are your weapons." Lavrin was given a new sword to accompany his sword from Hightenmore. It had a leather handle and a long thin blade with an engraving down the center. It was incredibly light and its end formed a sharp point. Two intertwined serpents were etched there, and the words above them read: **No power of evil can withstand the majesty of the Light.** The sides of the handle finished in decorative silver squares. The bottom of the handle had the same pattern, except the center of the square was an emerald.

Felloni needed no new weapons, so instead was given a special suit of leather armor which replaced his old worn one. Thick strips of leather were sown together overlapping one another, giving a strong and tight style.

Each soldier was armed based on his liking and skill. One young man with a thin frame and deep blue eyes was given a crossbow with a sling of bolt arrows to fire in it. He placed the armament snugly on his left hip with the container of its special arrows on his right.

Another older man with a look of honor and loyalty across his face received a long sword made completely of iron and he carefully sheathed it in its leather case on his back.

Kyra was given a small knife with an ivory handle which was only as a precaution. She received it gladly but hoped it would never be needed.

Each of the team was given a dark green slimy fungus to rub across all of their equipment and their skin to replace any smell they had with that of the plant. To most of them, it was quite disgusting in both smell and texture, but they knew it was necessary.

Lord Auden and Lord Denethor once more entered the dungeon of Saberlin to question Zekern on any knowledge of the Seviathans. When they saw him, he looked quite thinner, for he refused to eat anything offered to him. His hair looked greasy, his mouth hung open and he seemed in a daze. The rats had scurried into his cell and stolen his rejected food. Lord Auden smacked Zekern across the face to awaken him from his slumber. He tugged at the chains to try to retaliate but he could not. Lord Auden questioned him, "What do you know about the Seviathans?"

He grinned widely and stopped struggling in an instant. He began to chuckle, then laughed so hard that the lords stepped back. "You will never defeat them! You are all going to die and I will be free! No one can defeat the Seviathans! I will be free!"

Lord Denethor almost punched his smug face, but Auden controlled him. The lords left Zekern alone and both pondered if they could ever deal with such a prideful prisoner.

The group said farewell to their fellow soldiers and, all armored and prepared, set out from the city heading south. Lavrin wrapped one arm around Kyra's shoulders and the other around Felloni's shoulders as they left the city of Saberlin. Lord Denethor watched them and whispered, "May the King guide them."

Yet no one truly knew how strong of a foe they would be facing. How many really were there? Had anyone survived the attack on the refugee camp? Could the group beat this challenging foe?

# CHAPTER 5

# STURDY SRAYO

Now with Idrellon as one of their weapons of attack, the lords needed to decide the best plan of action. Since he had seen a lot as the King's scribe, Idrellon helped guide the lords through strategies. One thing they all agreed upon was that they needed to set out for Srayo immediately to use the time wisely.

The citizens of Saberlin waved to their rescuers as they left the gates of the city. The lords left few guards because they knew the townsfolk were glad to be back under the King's rule, and the only attackers on the city would come from Srayo, where they now headed.

The plan was devised. Around ten soldiers would be placed in carts and covered with straw and wheat. Once inside, they would open the gates to let the main army into Srayo.

Idrellon's first task would be to defend the troops sent to open the metal gate until they succeeded in opening it. This would need to happen quickly or their surprise advantage would be gone.

Next would be the citadel. The citadel had virtually no entrance except a small, locked door which was almost impenetrable due to the number of archer holes above it where the defenders could bombard attackers with arrows. Idrellon would lift the lords over this tall stone blockade and drop them upon the archers. Once the archers were taken care of, the main army would break through the door and enter the citadel.

Inside the citadel, there was one central road. Off this road lay ditches and bumps on which enemies would often trip and fall. At the end of the road, before the mansion of the lord, there lay a blockade so attackers would have to run at the barricade in two rows. This would result in an extreme slaughter of those assaulting.

Lord Denethor had come up with a way to bypass this defense. The main force would set up a box formation on the road which was a highly defensive but low offensive formation. Fifteen or so archers would mount the citadel structure and launch flaming arrows down on it. The blockade itself would not catch on fire, but the various trees and the grass near it would be in flames.

This would extremely distract if not panic those mounting the blockade. Those on the blockade would think that since the King's soldiers were in a defensive formation, that they were just meaning to force them out through fire.

Then the main force would shift to a standard formation and besiege the blockade. Past the blockade, all that stood in the way was the mansion which held little to no strategic defense. The city would be in the possession of the King if all went as planned.

Sadly, two problems presented themselves as a barrier to achieving this plan. One was the mountain pass. On the road to Srayo lay a single mountain pass, and although it was crossable, it would be an exhausting journey. Tired men made it more difficult to besiege a city. This pass was, unfortunately, the only way to reach Srayo unless they were to take several weeks.

The other problem was the task of convincing farmers to take in the soldiers. Farmers were plentiful, but they were often suspicious of strangers and would not wish to cart men into the city. If these two problems could be resolved, victory would be within grasp.

One thing was appreciated on the travel toward the mountain pass. The entire trek was on grassland. This made the voyage quicker and easier. The third day out of the city, the group passed through the town of Dreylon. The sun shone radiantly upon it, unhindered by any passing clouds.

Dreylon was a small town centered on trade. The marketplace displayed vendors down its streets, bargaining with customers over different wares and items. From food to weapons, fabric to cattle, the merchants of Dreylon sold numerous objects. Although the houses were in good shape and the town prospered, it was very cramped due to its small size.

To try to save room, many of the stores were actually extensions of houses.

Half an hour after they passed through Dreylon, a group of about fifty raced out from it to catch up with them. The leader of this crew yelled out, "Lord Auden and Lord Denethor, we must speak with you."

The army stopped and the lords met the fifty. "What is the meaning of this?" Lord Denethor exclaimed, obviously considering the issue of time.

The leader replied, "I am sorry to halt you and in no way mean to upset you. My fellows and I are highly trained fighters selected by the town of Dreylon. Dreylon has always felt in danger from the stronghold of Srayo on its borders.

"Ever since Saberlin tried to take over Hightenmore, we have been steadily training and, if I may say so, we have become an incredible force. I am sorry you have not heard of us sooner, but our people wished that we trained in secrecy. We already have collected our own weapons and supplies. We now wish to honor our town and our King by fighting beside noble men and leaders such as the two of you. Since we have heard you are heading to Srayo and it is the last major threat to our homes, we consider joining you the best choice." All fifty bowed before the two.

Lord Auden and Lord Denethor were both flabbergasted. Lord Auden finally managed, "The King of Light has showered down his favor this day. You may certainly come with us to Srayo and we are privileged to have you fight at our sides. You will be treated as equals amongst all of us."

The fighters of Dreylon soon mixed in with the combined team from Vanswick and Hightenmore. Their leader, a caring man with short dark brown hair, brown eyes and wearing a full suit of metal armor, paused next to the lords. "I forgot to tell you, my name is Warren."

Lord Denethor nodded and shook his hand. "Glad to meet you, Warren." Lord Auden also shook Warren's hand and expressed his appreciation once again. The now enlarged force continued toward the lofty mountain pass. Auden and Denethor relayed the plans to Warren who then communicated it to his men.

At the campfire that evening, as the soldiers rested for the long journey ahead of them, Warren suggested to the lords, "I have come to know many of the farmers who live nearby. Although many are mistrusting of strangers, I believe there are two who may help you. It would be much wiser to travel with men loyal to the King than any random farmer."

The army rested while Warren and the lords sought out these farmers. Voyaging to the first farm, the three discussed the best way to present themselves. The first farm sat in the center of a long, square field of wheat. Since it was the harvest season, most of the crop had already been chopped down and was ready to be loaded.

A black hound sat in front of the large stone house, and raised its head slightly. Seeing the men, it bellowed a deep, menacing growl. A short old man hobbled out of the house and wacked the dog with his thick wooden cane. He had a slight hunch and an angry stare from his tired green eyes on his wrinkled face.

Auden whispered, "Are you sure this is the right farmer?"

Warren returned, "I know he is cranky, but he claims to trust the King."

The farmer stubbornly exclaimed to them, "Why are you here, Warren? And who are these hooligans?"

Warren took a deep breath. "Sir, I have come to ask for a favor. In the past, you have said you follow the King. Because of this, we were hoping you could transport some of our men into Srayo with your wheat harvest."

"I am not here to cart around some strangers. Just leave me be to sell my crops."

After he returned to his home and slammed the door forcefully shut, Warren mused, "Not the reception we had hoped for."

The trio knew it was late and wished to rest their eyes from the eventful day. Returning to camp, they entered their tents and slept with ease.

In the morning, the three went to find the next farmer who had already begun his travel toward Srayo. He wore a straw hat, patched farmer's attire and a plain white shirt. He greeted them kindly as he walked his grey oxen, a piece of straw hung out of his mouth to the side. The oxen pulled a large cart full of ripe corn. Lord Auden asked, "Fine Sir, we wanted to know if you could grant us a favor."

He smiled, and his grin showed gaps in his teeth. "What can I do for you?"

Warren answered, "Some of our friends need passage into Srayo. We were wondering if they could ride in your cart?"

He looked back at his cart, and then at them. "Why can't they just go in?"

Warren responded, "It is a surprise. The Lord of Srayo's day of birth nears and they wish to give him a rare, special gift. If the guards saw them it wouldn't be a surprise, now would it?"

The farmer stroked his chin. "You do not need to joke with me. If I know anything about you, Warren, you would not be bringing a gift to the Lord of Srayo. What is really going on?"

Warren sighed then smiled. "We have gathered an army of the Light comprised of men from Vanswick, Hightenmore and Dreylon and plan to attack Srayo. It is crucial that we get several warriors inside the gates to open them for the army to charge in. You will not be in any danger, just drop of a few men and you can continue on your way."

The farmer stared at them wide-eyed. "Why didn't you say so? I will surely help you reclaim Srayo. I wish my family could see me know, aiding the great army of the King to victory. They always thought I was just your average farmer."

Lord Denethor tossed him a bronze coin, and within ten minutes, three of their strongest men and a woman from their group were piled into the cart. Lord Auden provided the farmer two horses to help the oxen pull the load. Idrellon was informed that he would have to buy the men more time because only four would be raising the gate. He understood. Denethor patted Warren on the back for his quick wit that allowed them to continue their task.

Later that day, the mountain pass came into view. The pass was long and winding. The climb up the mountain pass was tiring, but everyone found ways to keep up their spirits. Each person made sure they had secure footing as they continued. Thankfully, the trail was not too steep. If it had been steep, the rickety cart would have surely collapsed or fallen off the edge. Everyone hung as close to the inside as they could, and for good reason.

When the army reached the height of the pass, the sun had almost completed its decent downward. The sky was dark yet clear, and the last rays of the sun were their only light. The weary yet loyal soldiers shared one another's burdens as they journeyed along a small flat plateau at the top of the pass.

On this plateau lay a trifling town of miners. A lone tower stood tall in the center, used to signal Srayo with fire. This would become a major problem for the Forces of Light if lit, destroying all hope of a stealthy siege. Moreover, if even a single villager could escape and reached Srayo before the army, all would be lost. Utmost caution and precision had to be used to capture the workers before they could alert Srayo, then the army could continue onward.

Rich, grand fir trees surrounded the town. In nearby mines, shovels piled ore in large heaps. The sulfuric scent of the rocks mixed with the dense smell of pine as the noise of scraping ore clashed with the night's calm. It was fortunate for the attackers that half of the workers could be easily subdued because they were asleep. Also, those awake would only have shovels to fight against the heavy armor and broad weapons of the Warriors of Light.

The time for action had arisen. Six men, wearing dark cloaks and light armor, snuck ahead of the rest of the group. Tiptoeing past buildings and carefully avoiding stray branches, they soon reached their destination. The tall stone watchtower was quietly broken into and the six stepped up the spiral staircase. They bolted the door behind them and lay in hiding, three near the door, and three near the top.

Dispatches of twenty soldiers each marched to a mine with the intent to capture and contain the workers there. Violence would not be used unless necessary. The remainder entered the town and subdued all those sleeping. Hopefully, they could be tied up and contained easily, but the six inside the tower were ready to stop anyone trying to signal the city of Srayo.

Silently, the town was ambushed. At the mines, Lord Auden barely avoided a shovel swing meant for his head. Full of rage and shock, the miners fought against the Forces of Light. During their struggle, a few of the townspeople managed to flee. The soldiers, though, saw their escape and cut them off from the path to Srayo.

Thud! Thud! Men pounded on the signal tower's entrance but were unable to break in. The three soldiers at the door braced it, but the villagers began swinging their pickaxes. Soon they had broken a hole in the wood. From there, the door was kicked open by those outside. The three drew their swords and were met by numerous shovels. The tower defender by the stairwell gave an upper cut to the closest man with his fist, and then kicked him backward in the stomach. The other two defenders cast off their cloaks and rushed into the mob which had gathered, signaling the third to stay behind.

Against such a force, the two retreated back to the watchtower, scraped all across the face and sides. When the mob worked their way into the signal tower, the six defenders stood at the top of the building and firmly held down the hatch which led from the stairwell to the large pile of wood which would be used as a signal to Srayo.

Chaos spread like a virus and flared up like a forest fire. To and fro, everyone ran about: skirmishes erupted and pickaxes and shovels banged into swords and spears. Near the center of the town, civilians bolted frantically away from their pursuers. The women and children were captured and, though they struggled determinedly, were bound.

Eventually, all was settled as the last of the villagers were rounded up and seated in a large building. They were crammed together and watched by several soldiers. Some still wore their sleeping garments and had just now realized that they were prisoners. The rebellious miners, along with their families, were also held captive at this location. A few of the warriors were given the task of finding the food storages to feed the captives later.

Continuing on their planned route, Lord Auden could not help but feel sorry for locking up those people and instantly jolting their lives into panic. Still, it had happened and he must focus on the battle to come. Two hours later, the army reached the downward slope of the mountain pass.

Srayo was in view. It lay in a valley below the mountains, at the end of the mountain pass. From above, anyone could clearly define the citadel from the rest of Srayo. Houses were scattered within the wall. The citadel looked strong and well-defended and had a few trees growing within it, but what that seemed to stand out most of all was that almost everything was made of stone. The walls, the houses, even the lord's mansion was built of stone. Most windows were open except in the mansion which had colorful stained glass windows that shone with brilliance as morning broke.

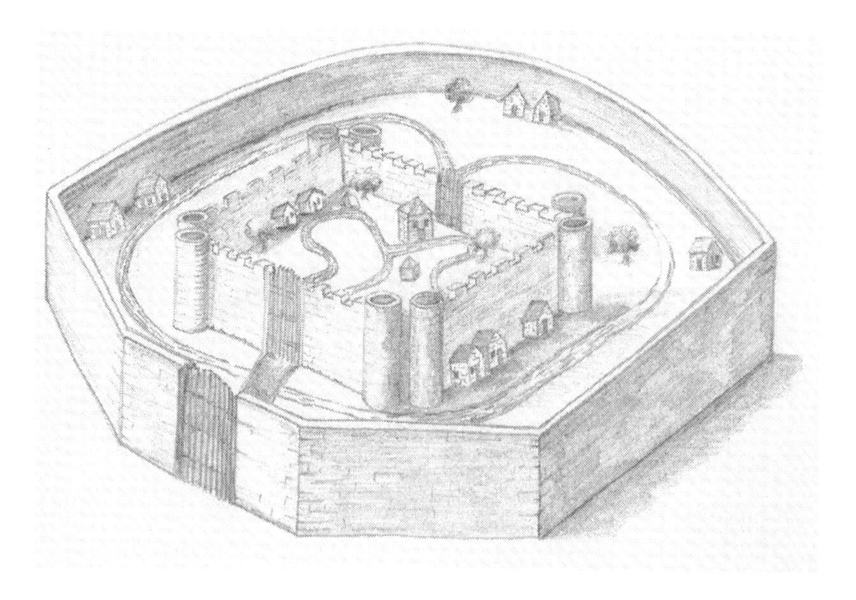

Lord Auden lifted up a prayer to the King in front of the army. "My gracious, glorious King. May you ever be favored throughout Amcronos. Please on this day grant to us comfort and strength to win this battle. We know you see our actions. I know you can aim our arrows to fire true and raise our swords to challenge the enemy."

The cart now clanked along toward Srayo and all the army was prepared to rush the key city. A change of plan had occurred, and the four had changed into farming clothes and acted as though they were helpers of the farmer. With his keen eagle eyes, Idrellon watched the cart moving toward Srayo and readied his wings for flight. The remainder of the army, numbering about five hundred, including the added fifty, hid out of sight behind large rocks and boulders next to the pass.

The guards let the farmer pass at Srayo's entrance, recognizing him. They dismissed the others as common workers or family members. When the cart passed the guards and stopped at a market shop, the four helped him unload the bundles of corn. Then they silently snuck into a nearby house which was unoccupied and collected a platter of food which had been waiting for them. The farmer went merrily on his way, nodding as he left them.

One of the four, a young woman, sauntered up to the doorway of the gatehouse with the hot, fresh food from a local baker loyal to the King. The woman was dressed in a long green dress with purple flowers and had her hair flowing neatly. The other three strong men crept to the sides of the iron door ready to spring upon the enemy. Luckily, they were well hidden by a few barrels.

The gatehouse looked like a large metal box with medium-sized windows on both sides. It had a flat roof and sat a few feet to the left of the gate, firmly against the wall. The three strong men had only the concealed daggers at their sides for weapons, and took each breath with caution.

The young lady knocked lightly on the solid, metal door. A small peephole flipped upward and two eyes stared at the delicious food in longing. Opening the door slightly, the tall man wearing black armor and a ring of keys at his side stared at her. She stammered, "I have come bringing your food rations."

He remarked slowly in a questioning tone, "You're early."

She started to turn, "If you want me to leave…"

He instantly opened the door, "No, no, it would be a shame not to take food from such a kind, pretty young lady such as yourself."

She blushed, curtsied and then walked in, placing the tray on a wooden table. Meanwhile a hand had caught the door just before it closed. Silently, the others crept in as all eyes were diverted. The man chuckled, "I wish I did not have to keep watch on the gate because…"

His statement remained unanswered as a dagger pierced his mid-back. The mouths of the other operators of the gate were muffled as they cried in agony from the unexpected but swift pain. The door was latched three times over and braced with the table. The four put on the metal breastplates, gloves, boots and other armor of the finished watchmen. Two of the men prepared to turn the cranks and lift the gate, the signal of attack, while the woman and the other man readied to defend them.

The magnificent sun cast shades of purple and red across the open sky. The large metal beams that formed the gate ascended. The army rushed down the mountains toward Srayo. Realizing this, the guards at the gate yelled for the gate to be lowered. The guards began to bang at the door of the gatehouse and demanded to be let in. Those who were not at the door tried to climb into the windows. The woman shot arrows at two men in the windows while the other man braced the door. Sweat beaded on his forehead and his hands felt cold on the solid iron. He bounced back from a thud on the door then returned to his position.

Suddenly, as the army rushed most of the way to the castle, the door was broken into. Just before a flood of enraged adversaries entered, Idrellon landed outside the gatehouse as they turned the wheel which raised the gate. Idrellon noticed the guards rushing toward them and flew up, slinging darts at those approaching the gatehouse. Their attention turned to the large eagle who was besieging them. Idrellon took an arrow to the wing as he fell to the ground, but kept fighting. One guard jumped on Idrellon's back and tried to jab a spear into his neck, but Idrellon flapped his wing, knocked him off and grabbed him with his claw, hurling him into the wall. The gate was up and the Forces of Light rocketed into Srayo. Yet things had not all gone as planned.

Srayo was now on full alert. Archers mounted their posts and guards rushed through the streets around the citadel.

Idrellon barely managed to grasp the lords with his claws and fly them over the blockade. As he dropped them, they attacked the archers. Denethor stabbed one, elbowed another off the wall, but failed to dodge an arrow aimed for his shoulder. This impact almost sent him off the wall but Auden gripped his arm with a strong hand and pulled him up.

In the streets of Srayo, skirmishes between the King's army and the defenders arose. The defenders had instantaneously rushed to the weapon racks and charged the foes. The men of Srayo killed many using a strike and run tactic and since they knew Srayo well, they took longer than expected to be defeated.

All was soon in place to siege the blockade, and the small door was broken into. Suddenly out from the blockade arose a large, snarling black bear. If this was not enough, the bear wore long sharp spikes, a few on his claws, and a few on his back. The bear roared in might and burst off toward the army which had just set up the box formation.

The bear bashed through its opponents' shields and slaughtered anything in its path. It took many arrows and cuts, but slowed little. Soon the force retreated to the wall upon which the archers were positioned. Idrellon, battered and bruised, knew he alone could challenge the bear, and squawked loudly in the air, drawing its attention. Idrellon rolled into a dive and the great bear stood up on his feet and bellowed, challenging the giant eagle.

Idrellon flew under the bear's claw swing and grabbed it with his talons. The black bear fought back by slamming one of the spikes on its back into Idrellon's side. Idrellon flapped back and landed. The bear turned toward him and charged the eagle; Idrellon barely escaped the charge by flying over it and unleashed a dart into its back.

The bear stumbled about in shock, and Idrellon took this opportunity to drive his beak into it and tackle it downward. The bear slashed Idrellon across the face, then across the stomach, but Idrellon injected another dart into the bear's neck and soon the beast stopped struggling. Idrellon hobbled a bit, and then collapsed onto the road. The doctors did the best they could to aid the desperate bird, and soon they stopped the blood loss as they bandaged him and took the arrow out of his wing.

The plan continued as the archers volleyed flaming arrows into and around the blockade. Yet many of the archers, although completing their task of setting ablaze the area, were shot down by the blockade's archers and fell from the citadel wall.

Those guarding the blockade scrambled about, shouting commands to put out the fire. The army saw the distraction and rushed Srayo's last defense. What they did not expect was that, by the time they reached the barricade, most of the enemy had seen their advancement, forgotten the fire and taken up defenses.

Now most of those trying to climb the blockade were knocked down. Eventually the fight moved into the blockade as some of the King's men breached it. The defenders were still outnumbered and though they had killed and wounded many, they retreated to the mansion. The Forces of Light followed behind them, led by Warren. Glass shattered as the invaders clashed into the lord's home.

Auden and Denethor descended from the citadel wall and ran after the army. By the time the two men rushed into the mansion, it now looked like a trash heap, piles of shattered glass and furniture lay in every which direction. Paintings lay torn on the ground and the mansion looked utterly horrifying.

Yet that was not what caught their attention the most. In the center of the room, they found the Lord of Srayo and ten of his top guards dead. Wearing long, dark blue capes draped over their silver breastplates, the guards grasped black dual sided spears tipped in red, and had masks of bronze over their faces. The lord though, displayed a look of fear on his open, clean cut face.

The lords left the scene and called together all of the survivors. Denethor counted that the victors numbered four hundred forty. Of the four hundred forty that remained, thirty were wounded. From six hundred seventy down to four hundred ten healthy and thirty wounded: these were depressing numbers. One soldier walked to the group with his helmet off, tears flowing down his face. In his arms he carried his brother, who had not survived an axe to the back.

Warren stood with a somber look on his face as he stared at the chaos that had arisen from the battle. Occasional fires burned, stone lay in heaps, and bodies were being carried along the roads. People fled about in shock dazed and bewildered. Had it really been worth it? He reminded himself of the value of owning Srayo. Not only did it seal off the entry of the minions of Natas to the Northwest, but it also was a highly defendable front against the adversary.

Lord Denethor walked over to Warren and congratulated him saying, “For your bravery and courage, Lord Auden and I have come to the agreement that you shall be the new Duke of Srayo.”

Warren stepped back and resurveyed the city. He was completely shocked, both at his becoming duke, and at the daunting thought of rebuilding this chaotic place into the prosperous city it had once been. “I am deeply humbled. Yet I cannot help but wonder how I will rekindle the flame in this city.”

Lord Denethor followed his eyes across the wreckage and destruction. “It will take time, but Lord Auden and I will always be there to lend our support.”

Lord Auden, on the other hand, was busy reading a letter which had just been hastily delivered to him by a messenger from the west. It was wrinkled and heavily damaged from the rain. This letter read as followed:

**Lords Auden and Denethor,**

**The most urgent of news. The town of Ken Van has begun a revolt. I have stopped most of it, but fear that I may need extra assistance. Supplies are cut thin and it seems the gangs of Ken Van are a worthy foe to face. I greatly pray that it goes well with the capture of Srayo and that, if possible, you might be able to offer some men to aid in my trouble.**

Your loyal overseer of Hightenmore,

Rando

Lord Auden shook his head in despair. He had greatly hoped that Ken Van would not rise to a rebellion, especially not at such a time as this. How could another town be pulled into the darkness? Auden remembered in the days of old, how Ken Van had started as a meager village. He would often visit his grandfather there. They shared many nights of apple cider and practiced swordsmanship. Yet the rising tide of black deceit had clouded the people of Ken Van as well. How he longed for this curse to be vanquished.

Lord Auden ran his hand through his hair and marched off to find Lord Denethor and Duke Warren. Ken Van had recently become a town of uprisings and confusion, since it had been constantly shifting between leading gangs. For a long time, Auden had wished to rid Ken Van of them, but they had always managed to escape his grasp in the shadows.

*****

Idrellon lifted his head as he lay on a large mat, but was not able to get up. One of the doctors applied a layer of gel across his wing and new bandages for his wounds. The doctor saw that he was awake and whispered gently, "Rest, Idrellon. We have won the battle. You need to heal because you have been deeply hurt, so please try to sleep."

Idrellon replied in pain, "I understand." He then laid his head on the mat and drifted to sleep. The other doctor then called out, "I need some help over here." The doctor who had been aiding Idrellon rushed over and helped hold down a wounded combatant as the doctor removed a sharp piece of broken metal from his leg.

*****

Lord Denethor took a deep breath. Lord Auden had just told him how Ken Van had revolted and now aid was needed to subdue it. The lords knew the wounded needed to stay at Srayo. Warren suggested, "I do not believe the enemy will be able to retaliate on Srayo before you can subdue the revolt. Take three hundred fifty of the men. Yet be sure to do so with speed." The lords gathered the army and set off for Ken Van with tired bodies but understanding spirits.

Warren began the task of governing Srayo with the sixty troops who had remained, plus those wounded. He rallied the people, and soon efforts were made to repair and clean up the city. He changed some of the cruel laws which had been set in place. Yet many of those who dwelled in Srayo did not help with the workload. They refused to allow Warren to tell them what to do. Warren patiently continued to set up trade and to return them to a comfortable lifestyle. He recruited some able bodied men to join his guard. Warren had also begun the job of repairing the mansion which was to be his home.

After the first week of work, Warren collapsed that night once again onto his silk bed in the mansion and looked up at the ceiling. He knew that the King was watching his actions. He also knew that the troubles which he had already faced, including the stubborn people of Srayo, were just the beginning.

# CHAPTER 6

# UTTER BRUTALITY

Lavrin whistled as they headed through the outskirts of the Forest of Bane to the west of the Mud Ridge Valley. The Mud Ridge Valley was an odd valley. It was mostly composed of outcroppings of red rock which stretched down a narrow chasm. It was the ideal place in which to hide a refugee camp.

A soldier walking next to Lavrin heard his whistling and questioned him, "Are you not the slightest bit afraid of the Seviathans?"

Lavrin stopped whistling. "No, I can't say that I am."

The soldier mused, “How is that?”

Lavrin raised his arm as his litz landed on it. “Because I know that no matter what enemy I face, the King will help me through it. I also know that I am allied with an extraordinary squad of warriors. To this group of warriors, I am so loyal that I would give my life, and I believe you would do the same.”

The soldier nodded and replied, “I do believe that each one of this team would forfeit his life for the good of another.”

Lavrin nudged the man. “If you are worried to face the Seviathans, take some advice.”

He answered, “What might that be?”

Lavrin drew his sword and held it in front of him. “Remember that with every blow you unleash, you do it for your family, your city and your King. Also remember that with every blow that is unleashed upon you, you endure the pain for your family, your city and your King.”

The soldier held his sword out in front of him, and then sheathed it. “Thank you.”

Lavrin replied, “My pleasure.”

Meanwhile, Felloni brushed pine needles off his face, and flipped his knife into the air, catching it as rapidly and as precisely as a frog would snatch a fly. He was glad they would be fighting lizards instead of men, because it made him feel like he was hunting. Often Felloni had chased down fierce animals when hunting, and to him this felt no different.

The trek past trees and under branches was a fast one for the group of twenty. Droplets of water rolled off the leaves and trickled onto their faces. Seeing the group was exhausted, Lavrin called for camp to be set up. With looks of relief, they eagerly awaited resting for the night. After a fire was finally lit, the tents were set up, and Kyra and Lavrin sat on the stiff grass near the warm fire. The other men had closed their weary eyes and lay snoring softly on fur blankets.

Kyra was dressed in a brown dress which had red stripes running down it in a pattern. Her hair was braided behind her into a long strand. Lavrin wore his usual leather ranger apparel over chain mail and, although the nights in the forest were slightly cold, he kept his hood down. He carried a sword at each side and seemed in no way tired from the journey.

Kyra turned her head and looked at Lavrin. "How do you really know the King forgives you?"

Lavrin thought the question through. "I suppose you know because even when we make mistakes, he loves us the same." He looked up at the night sky through the canopy of tree branches. "I think the King is more interested in your devotion to him than your mistakes. What he really wants is for you to passionately follow him with all of your heart and mind. Why do you ask?"

Kyra replied, skipping the question, "Thank you, Lavrin. You always know just the right thing to say." She got up and walked to her tent, knowing that a good night's sleep was always necessary, especially for apprentice doctors. Lavrin watched her leave and took the opportunity to enter his tent, close his eyes and begin to dream.

*****

When Lavrin walked out from his tent, he was embraced by the early morning fog. He wiped the sleep from his eyes and saw a large pot resting in the center of the fire. Felloni sat stirring this kettle. As Lavrin got closer to it, inviting smells of venison, potatoes, carrots and herbs mixed together into a boiling stew. Felloni held up his hand and said, "It has not finished cooling quite yet."

Lavrin almost left to begin packing, but turned. "Don't you ever sleep?"

Felloni continued stirring and remarked, "The art of rising early in the morning is a virtue which few possess. I find it most enjoyable, however."

After eating the hearty meal, the group packed up and set out. Soon the group left the forest behind them and began the descent into the Mud Ridge Valley. The refugee camp was cleverly hidden inside a cave within a rock formation. Reaching the refugee camp, Lavrin rolled open the stone which covered the cave entrance and looked upon a scene of utter brutality.

Everyone gasped in shock, and chills ran down their spines, seeing dead bodies lying across the floor and red stains all around them. Eyes stared wide open in a pure state of horrified disgust and astonishment. Blood pooled on the ground, and all the furniture and barrels of provisions were ravaged and broken.

Kyra knelt beside one of the refugees and placed her hand on his neck. She went to the next and the next, hoping to find even one survivor. She called out to the others after finding a paper under one of the lifeless bodies, stained slightly on the edges with blood:

Today is the third day of our struggle against the beasts which have barricaded us inside the cave. Our leader has decided we are to open the stone entrance and fight the creatures while our women and children flee out the secret exit. We cannot all escape through this exit because we fear the enemy will follow and chase us down. This would mean death for us all.

Yet if we stay and fight, they will probably forget the women and children and turn all their attention on killing us. I believe all is lost for us except the hope that our families will find peace. All the remainder of our food has gone with our families. This further shows the little hope that remains for us. I now draw my spear and wield my shield. We go off to fight a force of fifteen ravaging lizards that shred any in their path. The first battle we had with them left twenty or more casualties.

These lizards fight with weapons as if common men, but their yells can almost make a man deaf. Although they do not kill with every strike, they can endure large amounts of pain. This is due to the hard scales on their skin. Furthermore, they have tails of long needles which can be slammed easily into one's chest. One thing I have noticed, which I find odd, is that all of their weapons are at least slightly curved. I hope we can now be to them worthy opponents. May the King reign and his followers prosper.

After reading the letter aloud, Kyra looked at the results of the battle. Three Seviathans bodies lay dead among the possibly forty dead humans. A few tears rolled down her face as she recalled the time she had spent at the refugee camp. Now its keepers and defenders had been obliterated. One of the soldiers proclaimed, "How could anything be as brutal and evil as these?"

Kyra heard a moan from the corner and barely recognized the face of the refugee camp's leader. Long claw markings ran down his blood-covered armor, and all across his sturdy yet thin frame were scars and cuts. He sat with a spear through his chest and could hardly be recognized as still living. Kyra took out her medical utensils, but he pushed them aside. "There is no hope of saving me," he said, struggling as he grasped his chest. "Take the horn your group gave me. Make sure those captured survive. Fight Seviathans." His face rolled to the side and Kyra closed his eyes as he breathed his last breath of dusty cave air.

Felloni took the ivory horn from the man's belt, and remembered how about three months earlier he, Kyra and the others of their group had visited the refugee camp while Lavrin had been imprisoned in Saberlin. They had brought with them two children whose father had been at the camp. They were treated as heroes for returning the lost children, and the group returned the favor by giving the refugee camp's leader a horn to sound at times of trouble. Sadly when the time of trouble had come, the Seviathans slaughtered so intensely and quickly that there was no time to sound the horn.

The confusing part of it all was that the leader had mentioned that the lizard men had taken prisoners. Why would they kill so violently, yet take others as captives? It seemed as if the two actions conflicted with each other, like dark and light, forming some kind of gray. The bodies were carefully drawn out of the cave and buried in a plot of ground between the forest and the valley. The destroyed furniture was burned, and the cave entrance was concealed again by the stone door.

Upon the ground where all had been buried, a stone was placed, which stated: "Here lie the brave men of the refugee camp, who tried with all their effort to defeat Seviathan invaders. Those buried here defended the Mud Ridge Valley with honor. Although they lost their lives, their efforts spared their families for the glory of the King."

# CHAPTER 7

# RALLYING FORCES

Past dark corridors, up many flights of long marble steps. Past three sets of metal doors, through the miniscule light of flickering torches. Turning right from a circular library filled with books was a small room in which Natas sat on the cold floor. A pillar of smoke rose from a hole in the ground. Natas stood as an image began to appear in the smoke. The long crimson robe which he wore over his menacing attire hung on the ground.

The smoke swirled into a long, cloud-like wall which displayed the image of a large Seviathan. Natas's lips curled into a devious smile, and he spoke into the smoke wall. "Jafer, King of the Seviathans, how are my plans progressing?"

Jafer looked through his side of the wall with scorn and confusion, and spoke in shrieks and babbles which Natas translated. "You mean our plans?"

Natas replied, "I remember that when I first discovered your race, the Seviathans were divided. I helped your tribe rise to power and you to become the Seviathan leader. I united the Seviathans and formed the staff which you possess. The battles to set you as ruler of your people were harsh, and you would have failed if not for my intervention."

Jafer huffed, "True, but your army would hardly have had any weapons if I had not supplied the ore. I found the crystal which you empowered in my staff. Also, if it was not for me, you would have lost twice the men in the battle for Lake Tibern."

Natas squeezed his hand into a fist. "Do not forget your place, Jafer. Just make sure the plan is followed and everything is set properly. I will accept no failure from you, Jafer!"

Jafer turned and walked away from his smoke screen and began to delegate tasks to his managers and overseers. Natas watched as the fog column swirled back down the hole. He had great plans for the Seviathans. They must not fail him.

Jafer's feet stomped to and fro as he commanded his officers and troops. Some went to gather an army from the villages which they controlled. Others formed lines to make weaponry, the first heating the metal, the next forming the metal and the last cooling the substance. One thing which helped with the force's preparation was the fact that Seviathans needed little armor because of their tough outer skin.

Some Seviathans were sent in groups of fives to scout the nearby mountainsides, and to make sure no town had rebelled. The lizard groups were sent out and each headed in different directions.

Jafer smiled as the troops were gathered and armed, and gripped his ornate staff tightly in his hand. Next to Jafer stood his top guards, one on each side, heavily armed with scimitars and axes. From where Jafer stood, he could see Seviathans rushing in from all sides and gathering toward him. He knew the time was right.

# CHAPTER 8

# THE MAZARON

Felloni guided the group of twenty through the trees with intense speed. The forest almost seemed to give his legs new-found energy. The group struggled to keep up. As they ran, they ducked to dodge tree branches and sidestepped thick pine trees. Crickets chirped loudly as if in protest of the human activity. It took almost the entire day for them to cross the remainder of the forest.

Felloni stopped. The group soon caught up with him and, after catching their breath, they looked up and beheld the great Mazaron Mountains. Snow covered the tops of the mountains which stretched in front of them. They stood in awe of the majestic sight. The mountains were proud and tall, with trees outlining their edges. There was no path except a rocky slope which ascended upward. Although this slope was not too steep for climbing, there was always the risk of an avalanche.

Since little animal life would be found upon the mountain, Lavrin decided that a final hunting trip should be taken. The team set up camp, and then split into three groups of about six to seven each.

Kyra was content to stay at camp and study her medicine book. As she sat alone, she looked up at the night stars. It seemed to her that each star was interconnected with the others. She wondered how many stars really were out there in the depths of the unknown. As she studied the many procedures needed as a doctor, Kyra began to drift into sleep on the bed of grass under the moonlight.

Felloni and Lavrin, however, would have little such rest. They were chasing a deer which glided through the forest skillfully. Felloni launched a knife which barely grazed above its back. Rolling, Felloni picked up his knife, and continued the hunt. As the deer sped away from Lavrin and Felloni, the other four in their group lay in wait of the deer as a trap. The deer did not realize the trap in time, and the four jumped upon it from a cluster of trees.

As Felloni and Lavrin watched this, they remembered Macrollo. He had been their leopard friend who had died by a pack of evil hunters. They felt sorry now that they had killed the deer as Macrollo had been killed. Yet the deed must be done and the food was needed for the ascent up the slope.

The hunting parties met back at the camp and Kyra woke up when she heard them arrive. She jerked up into a sitting position, and then stood up, wiping the sleep from her eyes. Lavrin told her, "We have counted our catch: two deer, one pheasant, and three squirrels."

Kyra answered, "Very good." She then noticed Felloni sitting beside the campfire, flipping his knife into the air while watching a mosquito buzz around him. He did not try to swat it, just followed its path with his eyes. He gave no attention to his knife, flipping it in his hand as if it was natural to him.

Kyra sat next to him but he did not notice. She finally remarked, "Felloni."

He flung his knife into the ground in shock, as if awoken from a nightmare, and then turned. "What is it?"

Kyra turned her head to the side. "Why do act this way?"

Felloni picked his knife up from the ground and asked, "What way is that?"

As Lavrin sat down next to them, she replied, "The way you always seem to be in another world?"

He sighed. "I think it's time I tell you about my past." Lavrin and Kyra both leaned in closer. Felloni continued. "I was a shy boy growing up in the city of Gesloc, which was a very hostile environment. The water was dirty and the air unclean. Everyone in the city was protective of their families, so I had hardly any friends. Because I had so few friends, I would always imagine myself on adventures or in other lands. I did not talk often to anyone. No one would listen, anyway.

At the age of ten, my father took me on my first hunting trip. He taught me how to set traps, track, and most importantly how to survive in the forest. The fresh air, the cool river water and the forest's natural silence were so inviting to me that I never wanted to leave. I did not catch anything that trip, but it sparked my eagerness for other opportunities.

My only sibling was my one brother. Our family of four would work all day and rest at night, just to redo the same routine over again the next day. My task was to restock the wood in the fireplaces and kitchen stoves of a wealthy family. I would constantly be summoned to do my tasks and never had a day off, except the one hunting trip. In Gesloc, there are rich and poor, and since our family was poor, we had to serve the rich without ceasing.

A few years later, soldiers came to our home one night and tried to take my older brother into the army. My father did nothing to stop them because he knew that he could not convince them to let him stay. My mother was so furious that she left with me, leaving my father alone. Yet I wanted to be with my father because my mother was always bitter and angry, so I ran away from her once we reached the nearest town. My father was both glad and shocked to see me return. My mother never came back.

Soon after, Nadrian and Chan came to our town, and they were an interesting sight: Nadrian in thick desert apparel and Chan in farmer's clothing. They saw me sitting in a corner, looking at them. They were obviously lost and tired. They had cuts and scratches all across their clothing from the forest thorns.

They asked me if I knew where they were, and where they could find anyone who could lead them through the forest. I informed them they were in the city of Gesloc, and that I knew much about the ways of the forest. After I said goodbye to my father, we went north. I taught them all I knew of the forest, and they taught me all they knew of life on the island and the desert. Eventually we reached the Forest of Torin, and I believe you know the story from there."

Kyra patted him on the back with understanding. Lavrin, although sorry for Felloni, exclaimed, "Felloni, I believe that is the most you have said in your whole life!"

Felloni tried to force a grin, but really did not find the joke funny. Kyra saw this and whispered to him, "He did not mean it seriously."

Felloni whispered back, "I know."

A cluster of nearby bushes began to rustle and all eyes of the camp turned toward them. Lavrin's hand was at his sword instinctively. Suddenly, the fire went out from an eastern wind, making it dark. The entire group stumbled about, trying to get a sense of direction; when Lavrin heard a babbling noise from the direction of the bushes, he drew his sword. Vin began to growl and bark at the bushes, his fur standing on end. Lavrin yelled, "The Seviathans are upon us! Draw your weapons!"

Felloni drew a knife and unleashed it with a flick of his wrist toward the bushes. A loud shriek arose, obviously a sign that the knife had found its target. A torch was lit just in time to see five Seviathans leaping out of the undergrowth toward them, their teeth showing and curved weapons in their scaly hands. They were just as Idrellon had told them; they stood like humans holding weapons, but looked like lizards.

The leader held a whip in one hand and an axe in the other. The four other Seviathans each held a curved scimitar in one hand and nothing in the other. Yet even the open hand had the weapons of long sharp nails which could pierce skin.

The camp was flung into action under the dim light of the moon and the light of the torches. Kyra dove behind one of the tents and crouched there with her knife in her hands.

Lavrin held a sword in each hand and locked in combat with the master of the Seviathan team. The Seviathan swung its whip and its tail with accuracy and Lavrin, although dodging the tail, was whipped across the face. Lavrin reeled. Blocking the leader's axe, he swung across while spinning, but the leader leapt backward and dodged the swing.

Felloni knocked out the legs of his opponent with a side kick, but during the fall the lizard slashed his spiked tail across Felloni. Both fumbled back and regained their composure.

Sadly it fared worse for the other warriors who had accompanied Lavrin, Felloni and Kyra. Although they had advantage in numbers and they were all well-trained, they had not expected the speed at which the Seviathans attacked. One lizard man killed two humans in front of him with an upward slice then a downward thrust of his scimitar, but was taken down as two soldiers jumped upon its back. An archer shot it in the shoulder which gave time for a tall man with twin double sided spears to cross-cut its legs. Then, as it was already weak in the legs, a hammer connected an uppercut upon it. Yet the Seviathan managed to send its attacker sprawling with a forceful knock from its claw.

Felloni ducked under a scimitar and flung two knives to his side, one to the left, the other to the right. One missed, but the other hit the leader in the side, giving Lavrin a window of opportunity. Lavrin stabbed his sword into the beast's chest, punched it across the face and tackled it to the ground.

Lavrin felt long nails embedded into his side. He screamed in pain as he wrestled with the monster. Lavrin was in an onslaught of pain from the teeth biting into his neck and the nails digging into his hip. Angrily Lavrin kicked and punched, but he could not break free. Suddenly he noticed the Seviathan loosening its grip. He looked up through his distress and anguish, and saw Kyra above him with her knife through his adversary's heart. As best as she could, Kyra aided Lavrin away from the battle and behind a tent. There he could be safe and she could treat his wounds.

Felloni inserted one of his knives into an enemy's neck, rolled to the side and threw his blade into its chest. He kneed it in the stomach, chopped it in the throat and finished it with two blades jabbed into its back.

The two remaining Seviathans were still brawling against the team. One shrieked to the other and it completed a full flip, leaving its scimitar deep into an unprepared man. The creature grabbed the head of another foe, slammed it down, and angrily jolted its tail into the enemy.

Felloni sucked back his chest to dodge a claw swipe, then placed the enemy into a headlock, delaying the foe enough for it to be hit by three arrows. This meant one lizard remained. This lizard saw its demise and bolted away from them. It was first struck in the leg by a thrown spear, and then it was defeated by a warrior's swift jab with a sword because he could not move his wounded leg. The Seviathan called out an ear-penetrating screech just before it was eliminated.

To minimize the loss of blood, Kyra tilted Lavrin in an upward position, then, after applying cleansing herbs, began bandaging his wounds. Lavrin moaned in pain as she treated the bites which had been inflicted on his neck. Kyra tried to get him to drink some water, but after he tried to swallow it, his body rejected it and he puked it up. Kyra whispered, "Stay with me, Lavrin."

He rolled to his side, and some of the other men had to carefully carry him into a tent. Lavrin was placed on the cot inside and Kyra told the others to leave. After they left, Kyra took her tweezers and began to extract the spikes from his body left by the creature's tail.

Lavrin barely opened his eyes, and his hand weakly grasped hers. "Kyra?"

She smiled. "I'm here."

Lavrin closed his eyes. "How many did we lose?"

Kyra looked down sadly. "Five. You and two others are also wounded. We were very lucky not to have had more men killed since it seems they have fought and trained well together in the past."

Lavrin soon was retaken by sleep, and Kyra looked at him in sorrow before she left the tent. He was strong-willed. Kyra knew it could have been much worse for him as well.

The sun had now slowly risen, giving the group some light. Felloni sat with the other survivors and looked across the row of blood-stained armor. He then looked down at his own and saw it was also covered with dried lizard blood. Like human blood, it was a fresh red, staining Felloni's suit like the juice of rotten tomatoes. He cared little though, because such was common in war.

Most of the soldiers sat with expressions of depression and fear. Now they realized the type of battles which would be fought. Tears streaked down each face as they realized that they could have fought harder to save their comrades who now lay fallen. One soldier, who was an axe master with several axes held on his sides and back, stood up. "Although we have lost five fine men and others were wounded, the fight has just begun!" he exclaimed. "Now is not the time to sit around and pout! It is time to act! Let us bring the fight to them with all our might!"

The soldiers looked at one another, and then began to stand. Determination spread amongst them like a cure to a virus, and they knew in their hearts that the Seviathans would strike fear into their souls no longer. It was time to show the Seviathans the valor of men and the light.

# CHAPTER 9

# POISONED

Kyra rushed out of the tent in which Lavrin and the two other wounded soldiers were held. She held her medical book in her hand and flipped through it rapidly.

Felloni observed a look of despair on her face and entered the medical tent. He saw Lavrin and the two others completely green in the face and arms, and their skin looked as dry as a wilted flower. Felloni knelt beside Lavrin's bed. Kyra reentered the tent and knelt beside him also. She gazed at Lavrin's horrible state. "Do not worry, Lavrin. I will find the Perifern."

She got up and Felloni followed her out. "What is a Perifern?"

She flipped to the page and showed him a picture of a plant wrapped around a tree. It spread tightly around the trunk and branched out with golden leaves. The description read:

Perifern

**A rare mountainous ivy which has special healing qualities against poison. It wraps itself around sap trees which grow at high altitudes. It feeds on the fungus which develops on the sap trees; this helps the sap trees to grow. The Perifern is best used when brewed in hot water. Make sure the water does not reach a boil though, because this will give it an extremely bitter taste.**

Kyra closed the book. "We need to ascend the mountains and find the Perifern."

Felloni pondered, "How do we know the Perifern will cure Seviathan poison?"

Kyra closed her eyes, trying to blot out the question. "It just will. All I know is that the Perifern might be their only hope."

Felloni replied, "Agreed, but who will get it? Our troops need to stay here and recover."

Kyra nodded. "You and I will go into the mountains, find the Perifern, and return."

A soldier who was heavily armed with axes stepped up beside them. They remembered him as the one who had rallied the men the day before. He had a strong, bulky appearance and a small, square beard. His thick brown hair hung just above the eyebrows, and he wore a large metal breastplate made of sturdy iron. The King's emblem was carved on each separate piece of his armor and his helmet appeared almost too tight on his large head. "I could not help but overhear that the two of you will be traveling into the mountains before the group does, in search of a certain herb. I would be happy to accompany you."

Kyra agreed, "That would be magnificent. Three pairs of eyes are assuredly better then two. We will be leaving as soon as possible."

He bowed. "My pleasure. Tathor of Vanswick at your service."

Tathor turned and began to pack a sack full of food for the few days journey. Kyra appointed one knowledgeable man to care for the wounded with wet cloths and new bandages.

Since his helmet bothered him, Tathor took it off and placed it inside his tent. With his hood loosely hanging atop his head, Felloni carefully gathered his knives, while Kyra packed up her medical bag. She also carried an extra bag in which to put the Perifern.

The ranger, the soldier and the doctor headed up a path on the side of one of the mountains. They traveled lightly up the steep slope in search of the Perifern. Kyra felt the temperature drop the higher they climbed the curving path up one of the many Mazaron Mountains.

*****

In the camp, Lavrin's state grew worse as his green color darkened and his eyelids began to droop. Lavrin closed his eyes and tried to rest but could not, and fidgeted on the cot. The man tried to slow his raging fever but Lavrin's temperature rose steadily. Vin whimpered as he licked Lavrin's hand. Vin's tail hung low as he sat on the dirt and looked upward at his caretaker with beady eyes. He knew that his master was not doing well.

*****

The three helped each other up the path as a steady wind blew in their faces. Tathor looked down and grimaced. "Why couldn't these sap trees grow at the bottoms of the mountains?"

Kyra also looked down. She saw a great maze of mountains each tipped with white. The camp appeared small from their height. Her small eyes worked their way down the pathways of the mountains. How could anyone live in such a marvelous land which reflected the King's glory and yet follow the evil ways of Natas?

Tathor rushed ahead and scanned an old twisted gray tree. It sadly held no ivy on its trunk and seemed to sag, knowing its end was near. The strong bulky warrior remarked, "We should go back down. It has been several hours up this mountain and there is no sign of any of the plant. It might be best to search a different slope."

Kyra did not care. She began to jog farther up the mountain and noticed a blur in the distance, a tall tree with long boughs and a plethora of leaves. The three sprinted with high hopes. Yet it was no use; there was no Perifern. Still up the cold, steep slope they continued.

After two hours of traveling through bleak rock with little to no discussion, Felloni nudged Kyra and pointed his head up the path. She saw a long, broad tree growing right on the edge of the path. It had golden ivy wrapped around it, but unfortunately it hung from the end of its branches.

Oddly, the tree stuck outward and awkwardly hung sideways, so that most of it leaned flat over the edge of the mountain, as if it had been pushed over. Tathor was next to the tree, readying to retrieve the Perifern, but Felloni called out, "Tathor, let me handle it."

As Felloni neared, Tathor stepped back. "You may do the honors."

Felloni took a deep breath and paused. He studied the format of the branches, figuring how to collect the Perifern. Felloni took the first step on to the tree and forced himself to focus on the ivy and the branches, not the extreme height at which he stood. He strode like a tightrope walker and soon grabbed the first branch with his right hand.

He then crawled another few feet until grabbing a long branch with his left hand. He positioned himself in a stomach crawl and after carefully drawing one of his blades, reached the knife out. However, he could not reach the Perifern.

He crawled out a bit further, wrapped both his feet around two branches and stretched out both hands. He stretched as far as he could, slid his knife across the plant and barely grabbed it before it fell. Felloni slid his knife back into its pouch. He slowly turned himself around and crawled back toward the two onlookers. Kyra had her hand over her mouth in fear. Soon

Felloni reached the path and handed the ivy to Kyra before collapsing on the ground.

Tathor helped him up and remarked, “A fine show, my friend.”

Felloni gasped for breath. “That was a… a delightful experience.”

Kyra compared the ivy to the picture of the Perifern and was relieved to find the two looked almost identical. Tathor asked Kyra for the book and read the description of the Perifern. “Interesting.”

He knelt beside the tree and slammed his axe into its trunk. Clear, gooey sap flowed out of the hole. Tathor put a finger up to it and tasted it. “That’s definitely the tree we are looking for. Only mountain sap is that runny and sweet.”

Kyra packed the Perifern into her extra satchel, and the three soon began the trek down the steep, winding rocky path. Kyra urged her companions on as she knew that each step was a moment closer to the poisoned men who awaited them.

*****

Back at the camp, Lavrin and the other two patients tossed about their cots furiously, faring poorly. Their eyes hung heavily and small sores began to spread across their bodies. Their skin looked like forest moss due to the deep green color. They moaned loudly in anguish, but no one could help them in their pain.

*****

As the foot of the mountain approached, a lone Seviathan jumped in front of Kyra, Felloni and Tathor. It was a larger, stronger Seviathan than the ones before, and Felloni and Tathor immediately stepped in front of Kyra to protect her.

The Seviathan drew two spike maces while the other two drew their weapons. It wore long black gauntlets on its arms which were outlined in silver. Tathor yelled to Kyra, "Get out of here! Take the medicine to Lavrin!"

Kyra scrambled to the left, and the Seviathan did not even notice her. Its complete focus was directed on the two warriors in front of it. It flickered its tongue and babbled furiously, still swinging the maces.

Kyra ran with all the strength she could muster. She tripped constantly over twisted roots, trying to cautiously protect the Perifern. Luckily, she had worn a loose dress and kept her hair snugly braided. She knew time was fading and if she did not hurry, she would have let her three patients down.

*****

Tathor growled, "Stop your chatter, beast, and fight."

The Seviathan rushed toward Tathor. Felloni launched a knife into the enemy's stomach, but this slowed him little. Tathor ducked under one mace, blocked the other mace, but then was knocked down by the creature's kick.

The beast stood above Tathor ready to finish him, but swiftly Felloni rushed the Seviathan from behind and grabbed it by the arms. The lizard howled in protest, and while struggling to free its arms, attacked Felloni with its tail.

Felloni dodged its tail strikes twice before stepping down on its tail and locking it in place. The Seviathan now had its tail and arms held back by Felloni, and to this it shrieked in protest and fought the control violently.

Felloni exclaimed, “Tathor, I can’t do this much longer.”

Tathor charged the struggling lizard man, but it kicked him in the chest, then again in the face. Tathor got up and threw his axe at the foe, which sailed straight into its shoulder. The Seviathan launched Felloni off of itself and knocked its mace into Felloni’s leg.

Tathor drew another axe and leapt onto his adversary’s back as it plummeted to the ground. He then finished it with two axes deep in its back. Tathor let out a yell of triumph, but then saw Felloni.

Felloni lay on the ground, mostly intact except for a bloody and battered left leg. Tathor knew Felloni’s quick thinking had been the key to the battle. Slowly, Tathor eased Felloni upward and wrapped his arm around him to help him back to camp. Felloni winced from the screaming pain in his leg as they descended to the camp. Tathor reassured him, “Felloni, take deep breaths. We are almost there.”

Felloni nodded and within minutes they reached the camp. Kyra saw Felloni’s state and laid him in the medical tent. As Kyra began to aid Felloni, Tathor asked, “How is he?”

While continuing her work, she answered, "It could be worse. Although the gash is deep, no damage was done to the bone. If his body can compensate for blood loss, he should be able to walk in about five days. That is, with a brace on his leg for support."

Tathor sighed, relived it had not been too severe. Lavrin walked into the tent and knelt next to Felloni. "I guess it is my turn to watch over you, my friend."

Tathor noticed that Lavrin's skin looked rehydrated and his face was barely green. Tathor was amazed that the Perifern had healed most of the poison within an hour.

Kyra bandaged Felloni's wound and turned to Tathor. "Thank you for helping retrieve the Perifern. If we had been but an hour later, I fear all three would have died."

Tathor shook his head. "Do not thank me. Felloni was the true hero. I would not have lasted long against the creature without Felloni's assistance and quick thinking."

The three left Felloni to rest, and Vin joyfully ran up to Lavrin, jumping and barking. Lavrin reached down and brushed Vin's fur. Vin responded by wagging his tail rapidly.

Kyra went to check on one of the soldiers still recovering from the poison, and reached into her sack for her medical book. When she did not feel it, she scrambled through her satchel, trying to find it.

Suddenly Lavrin walked over to her, scrolling through the pages of her medical book. "I think you dropped something."

She walked over to him and commented, “I think you could read it better right side up.” She took the book from him.

Lavrin blushed. “I… I meant to do that.”

Kyra looked at him with a suspicious expression. “Of course, you did.” As Lavrin left the tent, he heard her quietly laughing before she returned to her patient.

Later in the day, the other two soldiers who had been gravely injured during the first encounter stayed with an unwounded man while the group headed onward. They had become too injured to battle and, although cured of the poison, still could not fight.

As the small band departed, one voice asked, “Can we do this? We have lost five men, and the other two who are wounded had to be left behind.”

Lavrin turned and looked each man directly in the eyes. “We have come to realize a serious truth for this mission. There are only two paths our destiny can lead us: success or death. This is non-negotiable. We have victory, or we die trying.”

Silence and despair was on each face, yet they knew they must give their all if hoping to survive their quest. Would the refugee camp be avenged? Or would more names be added to the list of those who met their end by the wrath of the Seviathans?

# CHAPTER 10

# TORTURE

Natas pounded his fist on the chair in frustration. Where was Jafer? Natas had never possessed a good sense of patience, and today he was in a foul mood. At least, more foul than usual. Jafer, although a good minion, did not have the best sense of urgency when it came to informing his master of the progress with the plan. Natas needed to know if everything was going according to the devious plot.

Smoke rose from the circular hole in the floor of Natas' special room used for communication with his generals, minions and lords across Amcronos. Jafer scoffed, "Why have you called upon me, my master?"

Natas replied, "Jafer, you know why. I need to make sure things are in order."

Jafer grimaced. "Of course. Everything is ready. We have over one hundred prepared and armed."

Natas smiled sinisterly. "Perfect. When will they be ready?"

Jafer retorted, "Soon."

The smoke vanished in front of Jafer and he made his way to the prison. He held his ornate staff in his hand and walked proudly in his gold and purple robe. Although Natas did not see it, Jafer considered himself to be almost as high and important as Natas himself. This did not mean he doubted Natas' power; he just thought higher of his own.

The prison was formatted in a long rectangle with one way in and one way out. This single door had one Seviathan posted on each side; they were tall, heavily armed and seemingly angry. The door of the prison creaked open, then closed as Jafer entered the stinky, filthy chamber. Long rows of cells walled in by multiple metal beams lined both sides. Each cell was fit tightly up to the next, and no windows could be seen. Only torches gave the dark room some light to see by. The sputter spatter of tiny drips of rain could be faintly noticed down the long tunnel of cells.

Jafer's personal torturer walked up in his dirty, blood-filled clothes. He was unusually short, and his back was hunched, making him appear even shorter. He carried a long whip that ended in a single spike, and carried a flickering torch in the other hand. "I have tortured him, Sir, but his will is strong."

Jafer grabbed him by the throat. "You have one job. That job is to torture answers out of people." He loosened his grip. "Let me come with you and see if you are doing your job correctly."

The torturer and jail keeper hobbled toward the chamber which held the reluctant prisoner. They passed many cells, each with no furniture, no window, and hardly any space. Several people were cramped into each cell, making matters worse. The man was chained to the wall, and his feet touched the hard dirt ground. His shirt was off and he faced the wall. His back was crisscrossed with stripes of whip marks. Fresh blood streamed out of these incisions, and yet no cry of agony echoed from the man. This was the special torture room at the end of the row, used for extracting information and punishing any unacceptable behavior.

It was a room larger than the others, because on each side of the man were long metal racks of uncountable devices, vials, books and odd weapons. The short, stout, cranky jailer preferred the long flesh-piercing whip that he made sure to carry with him.

Jafer exclaimed, "Well, what are you waiting for? Beat the weakling!"

The jailer whipped him repeatedly, but no words came from the man. The jailer whipped him again, but harder. The loud cracking and snapping noise echoed through the prison. The man cried out in agony, but then yelled, "Whip me as much as you like! I feel the presence of the King and he strengthens me! I dare you to try to outmatch the healing and hope of the King!"

Jafer growled, "Give me the whip!" He began striking the prisoner. "I will no longer tolerate this rash, stubborn, and ignorant human."

The man screamed through the pain of the thrashes, "I am honored to be attacked by the king of the Seviathans for the glory of the true King!"

Jafer replied, "Let's test that, shall we?"

He dropped the whip and dug his fingernails and tail spikes into the prisoner. The man winced in pain and moaned loudly. The torturer went up to Jafer and whispered, "My lord, if you torture him further, he will die and you will not have the information."

Jafer drew his nails and spikes out of the prisoner's skin, stomped out of the jail and slammed the door shut behind him. After the jail keeper left, the other prisoners who had witnessed the brutal torturing, asked, "How did you endure that?"

The man looked up to the ceiling. "The King of Light gave me peace, knowing that if I die I will be with him, so I fear death little."

One of them scowled, saying, "I've heard of that King of Light, and I don't want anything to do with him."

Yet the three others pondered, "How do you know he sees you and is real?"

The man smiled. "Every time I look at the faces of my children, Margret and Eli, I see the beauty of life which the King has given to me. When you accept the King as your savior, you can feel his love in your heart."

They thought it over as they stared at him. After a brief while, they replied, "We would like to have this light, too."

He looked over his shoulder, unable to fully see them since he faced the wall. "If you promise to follow the ways of the King and realize his love for you, the rays of his life will come into your heart as one steps into a room through a door."

They closed their eyes for a few moments, and then opened them. "Thank you."

The man cried out as the pain of his back returned. He longed deeply for water, but none was brought to his parched mouth. Yet somehow he knew that it was all part of the King's plan, and that he would have no more pain when summoned to the Haven Realm.

# CHAPTER 11

# UNFORESEEN CHANGES

Kyra rose from her bed and brushed, then braided, her hair. She put on her only other outfit, a brown and green dress, and after sliding on her leather shoes, she walked over and stood in front of Lavrin's tent which he shared with two other soldiers. Enthusiastically, she yelled, "Rise up, it's a new day!"

Lavrin, who had become accustomed to sleeping in his battle gear, slid into his high leather boots and was the first out of the tent. He yawned deeply and as he covered his mouth, Kyra commented, "You look a little sleepy, Lavrin."

He shook off another yawn and remarked, "Very funny."

Within a matter of minutes the camp was awoken. Sunlight travelled over the mountain tops and greeted the eyes of the tired combatants. Most of the men lined up behind a bucket filled with water which they either drank or splashed on their faces.

Suddenly, a Seviathan roar rippled nearby. The team readied their weapons and rushed toward the direction of the sound. When they arrived, they spotted two people fighting against two Seviathans. The Seviathans seemed to have the upper hand.

Lavrin called out, "Let them go, beasts!"

The Seviathans turned and one babbled to the other loudly. They rushed off up the mountains. They had either feared the number of opponents, or had decided to tell other Seviathans about the new enemy.

The two walked up to the group. One was a man armed with a longbow and a quiver of arrows slung across his back. He had wavy black hair. The other was a woman with long blonde hair and emerald eyes, who was equipped with several spears.

The man proclaimed, "Thank the King that your band came as they did! What is your purpose here?"

Kyra replied, "We have traveled here from Saberlin and have taken up the task of fighting the Seviathans. There is much to discuss, but I fear the Seviathans may return shortly."

The woman remarked, "I agree. My cousin Rowan and I have escaped a Seviathan village with four others, but they did not make it. I believe we would like to accompany you, because we also feel it is our mission to liberate the Mazaron."

Lavrin led the group out of the area to avoid further Seviathan encounters. Rowan and his cousin were invited to join them. They returned to their camp in a small grove of trees at the base of the mountains to finish their breakfast. The team and the two newcomers ate rabbit stew together, with the exception of Felloni, who had perched himself up in one of the trees, sharpening his knives.

The rescued woman told the group, "I forgot to introduce myself. I am Kasandra."

Kyra responded, "I am Kyra. I serve as doctor for our team."

Lavrin continued, "And I am Lavrin, once ranger of the forest, now soldier. Although we do not have a true leader, many consider me the leader of this group."

Kasandra pointed up to the tree. "Who is that?"

Lavrin sighed. "That is Felloni. I am sorry he is not eating with us, but he prefers solitude and deep thought. He is a fierce warrior and an expert with knives."

Kasandra placed her bowl next to the campfire as she finished and went up to the tree in which Felloni sat. She climbed up and sat beside him. "Hello, Felloni. I am Kasandra. I hear you are a knife master."

Felloni nodded. She resumed, "I myself prefer to use spears. Rowan and I have trained many months together to prepare to fight the Seviathans."

Felloni put his knives into their sheaths and looked at Kasandra. "Glad to meet you."

"So, how did you find the King?" Kasandra inquired.

Felloni answered, "Well, I would say he found me. I lived a life full of hatred and despair as I grew up. I was born and raised in the town of Gesloc, where my whole family had to work for our rich overseers. When I did not have work, I ventured into the forest. My father taught me how to hunt and trap, and what he didn't teach me, I learned on my own."

"Are you any good?" Kasandra questioned.

He returned, "Hunting is basically my life. I can track anyone or anything."

Felloni continued, "Anyway, soldiers eventually came and took my brother away for the army. Just as my family started to break apart, I met two people named Nadrian and Chan. I set out as their guide, and as I showed them the ways of the forest, they told me many things about the goodness of the King. Soon after, I realized I didn't need to hate anymore, and turned my heart to the King."

Kasandra smiled. "That is really amazing, Felloni. My story is not nearly as interesting."

He raised his eyebrows. "Every story is interesting."

She smiled. "All right, then. I was always raised to be smart and hard-working. My parents carefully demonstrated to me how I should behave. Rowan and I would sometimes play blind man's bluff and have other adventures. We strengthened each other in our characters and actions. I am so blessed to have a family who showed me the King's love at an early age. Yet I have always been a slave of those beasts and will put up with it no longer."

Felloni jumped down from the tree and Kasandra followed. Lavrin had directed everyone that they would have no rest this afternoon, since they needed to begin the ascent up the mountain to avoid any more Seviathans.

The camp was packed up and they began the journey up the northwestern side of the Mazaron Mountains. The journey was slow as the soldiers trotted up the rocky ground in their heavy armor. Both trees and animals became fewer and fewer. Luckily, they had enough provisions to last them for a while.

Rowan carried an unusually large load, insisting that it was the least he could do. Although Felloni wished to travel lightly and silently, he too shared the supplies. Rowan had found an interest in the litz and fed it an apple he had found earlier. The small dragon sat on his shoulder until finishing it then flew off and landed into Lavrin's sack.

Kasandra, unlike Kyra, kept her blonde hair unbraided; she wore a leather skirt over a layer of thick chain mail. Her spears formed an x across her back, and her leather boots outlined in metal protected her legs.

During the struggle into the Mazaron, there would be many a time when a comrade would fall and was helped up to continue the ascent. A strong wind assaulted the team and made the trek even less pleasant. Yet the sky was clear blue and the sun helped to delay the mountain's cold.

After the long first day, the group had trekked deep into the mountains. Camp was set up and the band rested. Lavrin sent out Felloni, Rowan and Kasandra as scouts to the nearby area.

They traveled further into the heart of the mountains and moved secretly between boulders. After a few hours, the three spotted an enslaved village which was ruled by Seviathans. The three neared it with caution.

The village looked shabby and run-down, revealing that the lizard masters cared little for their slaves. The three ran up behind one of the huts and extended their heads outward to survey the area.

They spied many thin people dressed in rags being forced to and fro by angry Seviathans. Some heaved bags full of ore, while others were sent to camps inside the mountains with pickaxes and shovels to mine for minerals. The three spied women washing clothes, preparing meals, and cleaning their wooden houses. The children also worked and were probably unschooled like many at that time.

Rowan whispered to the others, "It does not seem like there are many guards."

Kasandra glanced across the scene and counted five Seviathans. "That is strange. I didn't think they would have that few."

Felloni gasped. Rowan and Kasandra whispered, "What do you see?"

As he looked down an alleyway, Felloni asked, "What is that?"

Rowan beheld a large creature made completely of stone with large crystal eyes. It was chained around its arms, legs and back, and it pushed a huge cart full of stones. It was taller than the Seviathans by about two feet. Rowan's mouth hung open. "Is that? No, it is not possible!"

Kasandra remarked, "What is it, Rowan?"

He looked again and it was gone. "I have heard legends of giant stone beings called Stone Golems, which consume soil and are quite strong. However, I have heard there are only a few left in Amcronos. I never believed the stories, but that sure seemed like a giant stone monster."

Felloni's hand gripped one of his knives. "Follow me."

He rolled across the opening between the houses and crept along the wall. The others followed, confused but trusting. Felloni dove under a cart which had stopped, and then leaped into a hut with an open door. He ducked under the table, avoiding the gaze of a young girl walking out of the room.

He was soon joined by Rowan and Kasandra. Kasandra was about to criticize his rash action when he whispered, “I know what I’m doing.”

He crawled out from under the table, jumped through an open window and landed behind a pile of crates full of the meager food given to the workers. He turned his head both directions to check for prying eyes. He noticed no one, so he snuck through the passageway and crouched at the corner.

He poked his head around, and watched as the giant stone creature, standing about eight to nine feet tall, dumped the rocks he had been pushing into a pile, and then was escorted into a barn where his arms and legs were thoroughly chained to the walls. Felloni zigzagged across the dirt road, making sure to avoid being noticed by any potential enemies. He checked that his friends were still with him.

Soon the trio was behind the old, run-down barn where the stone being dwelt. They pried open the wooden boards and went inside the barn, stepping over piles of hay. The chains holding down the creature spread in every direction like the web of a spider.

Felloni crept up to the beast and put his hand on its back. He quietly remarked, "We are here to free you. Do you understand?" The Stone Golem nodded. Felloni motioned to the others to break the chains, and they worked silently to free the stone being. Soon most of the chains were broken. Once only a few remained, the Stone Golem stood up and tore the rest off himself. The being then turned and looked at his liberators face to face.

Rowan whispered, "We must be quick to escape."

The Stone Golem bellowed, "We must free the other slaves."

Felloni remarked, "In time. First, what is the best route of escape out of here?"

The Stone Golem exited out the back of the barn where the hole had been made, and soon the four navigated out of the town. Felloni knew they must move hastily before the lizards realized the Stone Golem was missing.

As they neared the camp, the Stone Golem scooped up a large handful of dirt and ate it. Kasandra wondered how anything could live on a diet of dirt and rock. She would prefer soggy bread over soil any day.

Lavrin stood up at the camp when he saw the four nearing. While many greeted the team, they were shocked by the new creature. Lavrin pulled Felloni aside. “What is that?”

Felloni pronounced, “It is the key to defeating the Seviathans.”

Lavrin put his hand on his forehead. “I mean, what really is it?”

Rowan walked up from behind and answered, “It is a Stone Golem. A powerful giant made completely of stone with eyes of crystal. It stands nine feet tall, a full two feet taller than the Seviathans, and outmatches them in strength and might.”

Lavrin crossed his arms and responded, “You can’t bring an uncontrollable monster, which you don’t even know serves the King, into our force without even asking me about it.”

Felloni answered, “It could be useful in a fight.”

Lavrin paused. “True, but you should have asked me about this first.”

Felloni quickly whispered under his breath, “You aren’t in control of me.”

“What was that?” Lavrin exclaimed.

Felloni turned and walked away. “What does he know about Stone Golems anyway?”

Soon the Stone Golem and the three scouts were fed and rested. The Stone Golem told the group that his name was Boranor, and that he was one of a small number of his kind remaining. Lavrin understood that they needed to leave before Seviathans were sent to recapture Boranor. The camp was packed and they set off heading east, making sure to be prepared for any sudden attacks.

# CHAPTER 12

# TRAPPED

Jafer stood inside his palace listening to a report from one of the enslaved villages. So the Stone Golem had mysteriously escaped? He knew he could not have done this without help. He then remembered that one of the groups of spies he had sent north had disappeared. He connected the dots and determined that some group, large enough to kill a group of his scouts, had also freed the Stone Golem and now was close to the heart of the Mazaron.

Two Seviathans rushed in and proclaimed, "We have seen enemies. A group of humans to the north, with two who escaped one of the villages, are coming toward us. They are well armed and must be dealt with immediately."

Jafer called his officers and ordered that eight Seviathans be dispatched to intercept this force which was believed to be headed east. They set out with speed and bolted off in the same direction as the group. Jafer twirled his staff in his hand and thought deeply. Did this mean more troops who follow the King of Light were heading their direction? Jafer realized that he would need to hurry preparing his army.

*****

Natas grimaced as he furiously read a letter from a guard who had escaped Srayo:

**To his majesty Natas,**

**Your Excellency, the city of Srayo, protector of the mountain pass, has fallen. The invaders were aided by an enormous eagle, and although we weakened them through our defense system, they now own Srayo and have sealed off the entrance to the Northwestern region of Amcronos. Srayo probably will not be recaptured easily, and no nearby towns or cities are prepared to reclaim it. I am one of very few survivors of this fight.**

**Your servant,**

**Otham**

Natas ripped the letter to shreds and cast it into the nearby fireplace. He could not tolerate such defeats. For too long those foolish Followers of Light had inched their way through the Northwest. Natas still owned most of Amcronos, but he needed to find a way to reclaim the steadily increasing amount of land owned by the King.

*****

Lavrin surveyed the rocky land surrounding the team. It had been three days since they had added the Stone Golem to their side. Lavrin knew they had to find the heart of the Seviathans and end their cruelty. Yet time was running out and he did not know if, even with the help of Boranor, they could last another encounter with the beasts.

Lavrin began to write a letter to Lord Auden and Lord Denethor, telling of the danger of the Seviathans, the villages under their control, and the need for help in order to destroy them. He slid it into the pouch on the back of his dark green litz used for delivering letters. Suddenly, a Seviathan's scream pierced the air. Lavrin yelled out, "Head to safety!"

The group fled to a nearby tunnel entrance to avoid the Seviathans. Lavrin knew they just needed time for the lords to send reinforcements. The pack of Seviathans leaped over a cluster of boulders and bounded after them. The team retreated into the tunnels, and Lavrin sent his litz off with the message before Boranor used all his strength to collapse the entrance behind them. This stopped the squad of Seviathans from following them.

Since little light penetrated through the rocks, torches were lit. Kyra counted everyone and was happy to find they all were there. While the tunnels were searched, Felloni counted the remaining supplies, and sadly found that they did not have much left.

Rowan and Boranor talked as they investigated one of the paths that extended farthest to the right. "So what are most Stone Golems like?" Rowan asked as he held his torch in front of him.

Boranor replied, "We Stone Golems are a shy race; only about forty of us still exist. We feed on the minerals inside rocks and soil, as you may have already noticed. Most of my kind live in hibernation within the mountains. I was awakened during the recent expansion of the mining grounds used by the villagers enslaved by the Seviathans."

Large gleaming stalagmites hung from the walls and the path swerved to the right. Shadows flickered on the ground from the torch which Rowan carried. The tunnel seemed to grow thin then widen at points because of rocks which jutted out of the side.

"Stone Golems are usually loyal to the King but are afraid to show it. We once ruled the Mazaron with pride and zeal for the Light but those scaly cowards put an end to it. It was because of them we fled and now live separated and isolated. Yet now I realize fear has crippled our hearts for too long.

Rowan contemplated, "Why are there so few of your kind?"

"The reason so few of us live is that Stone Golems only produce one crystallite in our lifetimes. These crystallites, unlike other gems, absorb surrounding ground until it forms a Stone Golem. Stone Golems do not grow or age like most creatures, but we eat to sustain the crystallite inside us. Most crystallites are red, like a ruby or green, like malachite."

Mushrooms grew in corners of the cave now and then. Rowan picked up a handful of large ones with white stalks and green tops, and then threw them down. "They are poisonous. Continue, Boranor."

"Occasionally, a blue one appears which is as pure and hard as jasper. Blue golems usually stand about a foot taller than most of my kind. My core is one of green and resembles an emerald. The saddest thing about us is we do not live together; I have only met a few others of my kind."

When some of the soldiers who had ventured through the tunnels returned, only one path had been found which did not lead to a dead end. The soldiers who had explored it said they had gone down it for a while until the heard a noise that sounded like miners. They had decided to return to make sure they were not found by those nearby. Lavrin determined it was probably one of the Seviathan mining camps where people worked endlessly. He realized this would eventually lead to a way of escape, and he wanted to receive news from the lords.

Lavrin knew well the incredible speed of the litz, so he expected it would only be a few days for the reply. Understandably, this put him in a predicament, because he had to choose between waiting for the answer but wasting valuable food supplies, or taking the path down the tunnel network to try to discover a way out. This could lead to another skirmish with the Seviathans. Lavrin chuckled to himself as he wondered how the lords would feel when he told them they had found a giant Stone Golem.

# CHAPTER 13

# REBELLION

Lord Auden and Lord Denethor had gathered their troops in the center square of Ken Van. It was the second day since they had arrived, and the leading gang who ruled over the town had made it clear that they would only follow the King for a price. This depressed the lords, because they had hoped that the rumor of Ken Van's revolt was just that, a rumor. Lord Denethor had spent three hours with the gang leader of Ken Van trying to discuss compromise and a peaceful solution, but he insisted upon a sum of five hundred gold pieces for their surrender.

Lord Auden had met up with Rando, overseer of Hightenmore, and they reviewed the current situation. Twenty men had already been captured by the gang members of Ken Van. Rando had troops on alert near Ken Van, and now waited for the response from the gang leader to Denethor's propositions.

After the debate, Lord Denethor relayed to Lord Auden and Rando that fighting against Ken Van was the only logical option. The price demanded was far too high and was impractical. Lord Auden understood, but was disappointed that the gang members had been so clouded by thoughts of their own power and glory that they neglected the Light of the King. He told himself, "It must be done."

All throughout the previous day, small skirmishes erupted between the cunning locals and the loyal King's men. It was now day two of the conflict, and the King's soldiers had taken control of inner Ken Van. They heavily barricaded themselves within all sorts of buildings, from inns to houses which surrounded the square. They braced the doors with wooden planks and furniture from within the buildings and patiently waited for the correct opportunity to strike.

One advantage which favored the lords was that their adversaries were often drunk and unprepared. It would have been a very different type of battle otherwise. Furthermore, those rebelling were far fewer in number than those who were not.

The advantage which presented itself to the combatants of Ken Van was that they knew the layout of the town, and were especially sneaky. Their numbers were not large but that did not mean they were not a worthy foe. Often soldiers were used to head-on battle, whereas in Ken Van they fought with stealth and wit. They hid in nooks and crevices and passageways throughout the town so no soldier of the Light could be completely sure they were safe at any time.

These facts played a large role in the strategy which Lord Auden had decided to use to stop the Ken Van rebellion. He knew the times of the week when the enemy was most drunk, and decided that would be the time to attack. He also knew that they would have to separate into small forces since one large army would be slaughtered from all sides.

Lord Auden had heard from an inside source loyal to the King of Light that tonight there would be a large festival in Ken Van where many were likely to get incredibly drunk. It was the time to strike. If the gang leaders were intoxicated, it was the best chance the Forces of Light had.

It was now one hour away from this festival, so the bands of soldiers prepared their weaponry, studied their course of action, and spread black soot across their armor for camouflage under the dark night.

The festival would occur throughout Ken Van, so each band would search a certain area. Once found, they would engage rapidly, unless they discovered a force larger than their own. In that case, they would find help from another group and take the force out together.

When the time struck, each group snuck out of the buildings and worked their way to their positions. The search began. Lanterns were lit in each house, providing little darkness in which to creep. Still, the Men of Light managed. Suddenly, a cry was heard from the northern part of town. The battle had started. Lord Denethor with his team of five others fought a party of five rogues. These rogues wore light armor so they were a lot more maneuverable, but had poor aim because of the brandy.

It was difficult for the Forces of Light to catch the scoundrels since they could disappear through secret alleyways or hide in places the soldiers could not reach. Many of the rebellious men leapt upon their own roofs and used the upper ground. While the gang members threw weapons down upon the soldiers, Lord Auden's and Denethor's archers returned the volley.

Lord Denethor's eyes caught the leader of the rebellion, who rushed through the street, killing several with his two short swords. The man had a long black mustache, and wore a flat helmet which sat over his intense brown eyes. Lord Denethor sped up to him and fought him furiously. Lord Denethor twirled his long sword brilliantly, while the gang leader stabbed aggressively with his shorter swords.

The two dueled with skill. Lord Denethor blocked a slice, tripped his opponent with a kick from his right foot and quickly placed the tip of his sword on the man's neck. The gang leader lifted his hands as a sign of giving up. The defenders surrendered also and were tied up. Some pledged to live as ordinary citizens and were let go. Others, whose hearts were filled with stubbornness and pride, refused to follow the King and were sent to Saberlin.

Ken Van was a town full of confusion in the days to follow. Lord Denethor looked up into the sky and saw a small blur. When it neared, he noticed the small, scaly figure as

Lavrin's litz. He knew from the direction which it had come that it was sent from the Mazaron.

The litz landed on his arm, and Denethor took it to Auden who lay on a small white bed, trying to recover his strength from the battle. Auden sat up and greeted Lord Denethor. Denethor carefully withdrew the parchment and handed it to him. Auden read it aloud:

To Lords Auden and Denethor,

We have ventured into the Mazaron to find the Seviathans. My group has lost about half in the struggle against them and they are a force to be reckoned with. We have picked up a few helpers along the way - two village escapees and one giant Stone Golem named Boranor. We have killed a few Seviathans, but fear we will need help because there are probably more of them. They have thick skin, spiked tails and curved weapons as told by the King's scribe. They stand about seven feet tall and can withstand more than expected. Our supplies grow thin as we try to find their weaknesses, but we will continue our mission.

Your friend and soldier,

Lavrin

The two glanced at each other. This was not at all what they had expected. They had thought there were only a few Seviathans, not more than those sent could handle. Moreover, the team had discovered a Stone Golem, a creature of myth or legend. They knew they still had four hundred left after squashing the rebellion, and wondered if they might need additional support from Srayo.

Denethor left Auden to rest; he knew order must be established in Ken Van before plans were made to help fight the Seviathans. He gathered with all the townsfolk in the square and declared, "People of Ken Van. Men and women, farmers and merchants, people of all trades. I have come to tell you two new laws which will be enforced. You have been freed from the rule of the gangs and now are under the care of the King of Light. He will protect you and you will live in goodness. There shall be no more slavery in the town, and each person will be limited to one cup of wine, beer or brandy a day. I pray that each of you will know the ways of the King. Thank you."

Auden got up from his rest and joined Denethor as they went to visit the scribe in Ken Van, who had given Lavrin and the others a copy of the King's histories. He was the one who had penned the same book that Lord Auden had read to the soldiers at Hightenmore.

They walked up to the small but sturdy house and knocked on the door. The door was opened by a slightly small man with a slim body and blonde hair. He wore a simple brown, common robe, but exhibited a warm smile. "Come in. Sit down, I insist. My name is Matthias. I hope you will enjoy my work. I have heard of the victory in the town, it is good to hear Ken Van has finally been freed."

The two entered the shelter and sat on ordinary wooden chairs at a table across from the scribe. Next to them was a bookshelf crammed full of quills, ink and papers. Beside the study they were in, only a neat kitchen and a simple bedroom could be seen. A small bed with a black blanket stood with a night stand to its right. On the table in the study were three books which looked identical to one another. Lord Auden brought out their copy of the King's Histories and compared it to the three. They matched perfectly.

Lord Denethor scrolled through one of the books as Lord Auden returned their copy to its pouch. Denethor marveled at the skilled writing and the descriptive pictures within the book. He remarked to the scribe, "This is fine craftsmanship."

Matthias' smile widened. "Thank you, kind sir."

Lord Denethor closed the book. "May I take this to display in the halls of Vanswick for all to see?"

Matthias remarked, "My pleasure."

Auden looked at Denethor and nudged his head toward Matthias. Lord Denethor understood the motion and asked the writer, "Matthias. My comrade and I have important matters to attend southward, but have no one to lead the town of Ken Van until we return. We were wondering if you would do this for us."

Matthias stared at them with eyes wide open, "Why would you consider me? I am but a scribe."

Auden replied, "You are a talented man who knows a lot about history, so you will probably avoid the mistakes of old. You are humble and you deeply love the King. Is this not enough reason? This will only be for a short while, no more than two weeks."  Deeply honored, Matthias got up and began to ready himself for the task.

The two lords left the new leader to begin their own task. They sent a message to Srayo for reinforcements and also returned the litz back with a message saying they were on their way.  The mission to defeat the Seviathans would sadly be more dangerous than anyone could imagine.

## CHAPTER 14

# THE MINING CAMP

Two days passed before the litz returned to Lavrin. He stroked it and then took the message from it. It was written:

Dear Lavrin and our selected team,

We have heard of your struggles against the Seviathans. Srayo has been successfully captured and we now head to your aid. Continue to fight against them until we can arrive. I hope you will stay strong and focused. May the King ever bless your efforts.

Your Faithful Lords,

Auden and Denethor

He told the others that help would soon be on the way. Now they needed to decide whether to stay put and wait for them, or leave the tunnels but risk having to fight the Seviathans before help arrived.

The team chose to vote on the matter. Out of fifteen, nine voted to leave, which left six with the decision to stay put. Felloni and Boranor were two of those who wanted to risk fighting, while Lavrin and Kyra wished to wait for help.

Although displeased, Lavrin agreed to travel down the tunnel and find out where it might lead – hopefully, out of the mountain. Everyone packed up and journeyed down the dark, damp tunnel. Soon they began to hear voices nearby.

Felloni motioned for the group to stop and, getting down on his stomach, he crawled out slightly to find where the voices were coming from. He crawled out several feet and a large hole in the side of the cave opened up.

He observed a mining camp, where a line of workers stood next to a wall of rock and swung at it with pickaxes in rhythm. Seviathans towered behind them, whipping them when they started to slack. The moans of overworked men and women mixed with the crackle of the whips, creating a gruesome scene.

Other Seviathans patrolled the site, supervising those who pushed the full carts out or pushed empty carts in. Felloni crawled back and reported to Lavrin, "It is a Seviathan mining camp. There are about four overseers that I can see, and about three more who are whipping the slaves. The workers are weak and are being abused. If we do it correctly, I think we can hit them before they know what's coming."

Lavrin nodded and walked up to the side of the hole. The group waited until he motioned that the Seviathans were not watching. They then rushed into the mining camp with weapons drawn and caught the beasts by surprise. All of the workers dropped to the ground against the wall, afraid to be caught in the fight.

Boranor jumped upon a Seviathan and slammed it with a two-handed pound. He then grabbed it by the arm and launched it at another lizard. They both fell from the attack, although they somehow managed to survive it.

Felloni ducked his head under a Seviathan arrow, and completed a double crossing motion with his blades, which slashed a foe in the chest. The adversary shrieked in rage, then dashed at Felloni with hands extended and mouth open, displaying his sharp teeth. The Seviathan's tail swerved rapidly; the tips of the spikes on its tail were a bright green, obviously poisonous.

Lavrin, on the other hand, blocked a spear thrust, sliced his enemy in the legs, then head-butted him. This he instantly regretted since he had not perceived Seviathans would have such thick skulls. The Seviathan thrashed Lavrin across the chest with its axe.

Kasandra thrust one of her spears through the stomach of her opponent then another soldier ran his chain mace down onto its head. It sank to the ground dead, crimson blood flowing from its body. Kasandra then turned and spied Rowan engaged with an adversary who looked to have the upper hand. She quickly bolted toward them to assist her friend.

Boranor wrestled with a Seviathan who had jumped upon his back. Boranor grabbed the lizard and tossed it onto the solid earth, then stomped on it with his massive stone foot. The creature struggled violently, clawing at Boranor's foot and stabbing him with its poisoned tail. The scratching and biting affected Boranor little and the poison was harmless since he was made of rocks. Boranor grabbed a large boulder and smashed it into the struggling Seviathan's head, finishing it.

Felloni stared into the eyes of his adversary, trying to read its thoughts like the charts of a map. Felloni battled one on one with the beast since the others were preoccupied. Felloni held a knife in each hand, blades extending outward. He rolled away from the foe's pounce and slung a knife at its side. The Seviathan was too quick, and grabbed the blade by the handle. He cast it to the side and continued toward him. One soldier came alongside, cutting open the creature's hand with his sword, but was bit in the leg and collapsed to the ground.

Lavrin fought his opponent with the help of Tathor. The two surrounded the lizard and attacked from both sides. The Seviathan was quick and either blocked or dodged their efforts to strike it. It carried two long hammers, but also had its natural weapons of teeth and tail. The beast inflicted a hammer pound on Tathor's left shoulder, but he tossed the axe in his other hand into the creature's back. This gave Lavrin the opportunity to punch it across the face with his left hand, and then thrust his sword into its heart with the other.

Rowan stumbled backward as his enemy was about to inflict a sword slam. Out of nowhere, Kasandra tackled it to the rocky floor and stabbed a spear into its leg. The Seviathan quickly removed it before scrambling back to its feet. Although it took Kasandra longer to return to her regular position, Rowan was ready. He shot two arrows quickly, both landing in the lizard's throat. The lizard bounded about, grabbing at the arrows piercing its neck. As it did so, another soldier met it with an axe in its side. The fiend was finished.

The combined forces of the humans and the Stone Golem were too much for the Seviathan slave masters, and soon the Seviathans controlling the mining camp were no more. Rowan noticed something interesting as he surveyed the dead lizards. Each one wore a red crystal on a golden chain around its neck, which he thought he had seen on the other Seviathans they had encountered earlier. He guessed that it was a symbol of Seviathan pride or some other gesture. Maybe it meant they were trained as warriors; he was not sure.

As the workers were set free and the area was scoured for any possible food, Kyra treated her wounded patients. Tathor had suffered a blow from a hammer, Lavrin was bleeding from the axe marks, and a few other soldiers had various injuries. She gently applied a bandage wrap around Lavrin's mid-chest; luckily it had not wounded any weaker part of his chest, like his heart.

After Lavrin was done being treated, Vin began to bark loudly. Standing next to Vin was an average-sized man with a unruly beard and tough arms. He wore simple worker's leggings and shirt, yet seemed oddly familiar. Vin continued to bark as Lavrin and older man stared questioningly at one another, trying to remember the stranger in their presence. Then a thought flashed into Lavrin's mind. Was it possible? Could it be his long lost father had been found in a Seviathan mining camp? The gleam in Lavrin's eyes suddenly alerted his father, as tears rolled down both faces. It had to be! It just had to be!

They ran up to one another and embraced, as a river of tears flowed from the oceans of their eyes. Both sputtered for words, but for a short while none were found. Everyone around them watched in a confused yet somehow understanding manner; father and son had been reunited. Kyra walked up to find Lavrin tightly hugging his father, happy and relieved after so many long years.

Lavrin stuttered, "Father, Father, is it really you?"

His father replied, "Yes, my son."

Everyone around them thought it best to leave them alone for a while until they gained their composure. They gathered and counted the food and searched the mining camp for other useful items. The miners had been set free but chose to stay with the soldiers, until they moved to a safer area.

"I have missed you so much, Father," Lavrin cried.

"I have missed you more than words can express," Lavrin's father returned.

Lavrin then questioned, "What happened to you? I thought you had died in the fire."

"It is a long story," his father answered. "Your mother and I were dragged out of the house before they set the fire, and we were tied up and taken into the mountains for slave labor. After a year of working, your mother was taken out of the mountains by smugglers of Natas who headed in the direction of Balyon. That is where I believe she is now, but I cannot be sure. I only hope she has found a better life than I have experienced here."

Lavrin paused. "Do you think she is alive?"

His father sighed. "I do not know, my son, but I do know you've proven yourself to be quite the warrior."

Lavrin then believed it would be fitting for his father to meet the team of soldiers. He started by introducing him to Felloni. "My father, this is my comrade who has incredible skill with knives." The two shook hands and Felloni remarked, "Lavrin has commented often that you loved the King with all your heart. I am glad to hear that."

Lavrin continued on to Kyra. "This is Kyra, our band's doctor, who has a loving heart and an understanding mind."

Lavrin's father shook her hand. "Glad to meet you, young lady."

She responded, "Nice to meet you, sir."

Lavrin's father replied, "No, please call me Gevnor."

As they walked onward, Gevnor told his son, "You have found quite the lady for yourself, my son." Lavrin looked at him awkwardly then laughed.

Lavrin introduced him to Boranor, Tathor and the rest of his team. They then caught up on everything which had happened since the day of their separation. Lavrin shared of his adventures in the Northwest and of his capture in Saberlin. He then told of his quest into the Mazaron and the encounters with the Seviathans. Gevnor listened proudly to the tales his son shared of his victories for the King.

Gevnor then painfully told of his long days in the mines and the constant whippings he received during his work. He recalled that he had seen Boranor hauling away the carts of ore and rock, but had never been able to talk to him. He scorned himself that he could not have kept Lavrin's mother with him, and did not know anything of her whereabouts. Lavrin understood, knowing his father had tried his best.

When they finished their conversation, Lavrin saw Vin scurrying around with a few older children who looked ragged and unfed. The group offered them some food, which they received gladly. The team knew they needed to get out of the tunnels to bring the miners to safety, so they started down the path which was used to push the carts.

The group made its way to the tunnel exit and right as they neared it, they found a group of eight Seviathans standing at alert, ready to kill. Tathor groaned, "When do they ever stop coming?"

Quickly, the workers were moved backwards out of the way of the fight, and the soldiers went out to meet them. The lizards communicated amongst one another with loud babbles while the forces engaged.

The clash of metal ricocheted down the thick tunnel walls as the two squadrons burst into battle. Boranor was the first to reach the Seviathans, and with a mighty roar that was so deep few creatures could have bellowed it, he charged at the lizards.

Within moments, casualties mounted from both sides as arrows sped and swords clanged while the battle raged. Kasandra launched spears at her foes, and Lavrin fought bravely against a snarling enemy. Kyra dragged a wounded man from the onslaught and tried to slow the seeping blood from his arm.

Felloni parried an axe and dodged an arrow before stabbing a Seviathan in the back of its leg. It screamed in agony as it collapsed, still alive but unable to stand. Felloni then dove over the beast and cut it across its throat. Sadly, this left him unaware of a spear swing, and he fell to the ground in pain.

Rowan was swift to cover for Felloni with rapid fires from his bow. Felloni got up and staggered back past the line of soldiers. Kyra helped him make his way to the wide part of the tunnel.

Boranor swung his arms with intense force and knocked a Seviathan off its feet. Yet he was not totally unthreatened - two Seviathans jumped at him from both sides and dragged him downward. A brave soldier launched his shield into one of them and Boranor took the chance to shake off their grip. Lavrin called a retreat, seeing their adversaries gaining the upper hand.

Oddly, the six remaining Seviathans did not follow their retreat into the tunnel, but waited at the tunnel entrance. It seemed the lizards wished to starve out the humans more than try to slaughter them in battle. The group set up camp and counted their men and their remaining provisions. Luckily, the food from the camp would last them for a while, but on the other hand, six men had been lost. This left nine soldiers, waiting for reinforcements from the lords.

Those from the mining camp told Lavrin, "A few of our men can stay with you and fight, but the others must accompany the women and children to safety."

Lavrin replied, "That is very kind of you, and would be much appreciated." Eight men were then given spare weapons and armor and added to their side.

Lavrin walked down the tunnel to try to clear his head, but found Felloni standing there with arms crossed. Felloni sternly grumbled, "I know you won't agree to this, but we need to attack them now when they don't expect it."

Lavrin ran his hands through his hair, stressed and overwhelmed by the current situation. "Felloni, I just can't agree to that. We all need to relax and just gather our strength."

Felloni left Lavrin alone, knowing he could not change Lavrin's mind. He headed toward the tunnel exit with determination. He focused little on the surrounding. The occasional bat descending from the dark ceiling did not enter his mind. The occasional gray mushrooms and few hanging stalagmites were not in his focus. Squinting in the dim light, Felloni's eyes were directed on the path in front of him. Although they did not read hatred, they shone with intensity and willpower.

Rowan detected Felloni approaching and stood up beside him. "Where are you going at this time of night?"

He turned to him. “Lavrin is trying to let the men recover, but the Seviathans are unprepared. I do not care if I have to go alone, I will kill as many as the King allows.”

Rowan said, “I am coming with you.”

Boranor exclaimed behind them, “I as well.”

Felloni turned and continued toward the enemy. He knew the two would help drastically, but did not feel like thanking them for their eagerness to aid him.

While their teammates nursed their bruises, the three headed off: an archer, a knife master and a stone giant setting out to battle a pack of violent lizard men. One of the soldiers barely overheard the conversation and rushed to Lavrin to inform him. Lavrin instantly gathered the remainder of the group and marched after them.

Felloni, Rowan and Boranor stopped and crouched behind a part of the cave wall and counted six Seviathans. Rowan loaded his bow and, pulling the string back to his ear, launched an arrow at an unprepared lizard, nailing it in the chest. The three then dashed out of hiding toward the adversaries with weapons extended. Rowan climbed onto Boranor’s back and unleashed arrows from atop him.

Within the tunnels, Lavrin heard the roar of Boranor mixed with the clash of metal. He prayed to the King that they would survive long enough for him and the rest of the force to reach them.

Felloni sidestepped a kick, and then sliced the beast's hand. He slid under the creature's legs and pulled its tail, causing it to collapse on the ground. Felloni ducked under the swing of a sword, but then was slammed in the back by a spiked tail. He continued to fight, but was weakened.

Boranor grabbed a Seviathan mace and tossed it aside. Abruptly, Boranor was attacked from all sides and bellowed in pain. Understanding the situation, Rowan shot one of the three in the mouth, then jumped off Boranor and tackled another to the ground. Both lizard and human were injured from this crash.

Boranor, glad to be released from the struggle, smacked the other lizard with his forearm using every ounce of his strength, and it collided with the side of the wall. Lavrin drew his swords and dove into combat with fury.

Lavrin found himself next to Rowan, who remarked, "So you came after all." Lavrin blocked a downward swing which freed Felloni to stab the foe in the stomach. Another man kicked him in the leg and Lavrin finished it within moments.

Felloni tossed a knife to Rowan, who had lost his bow. Rowan caught the knife and stopped the lizard's tail from knocking into him. This beast was then pounded by a downward hammer and embedded by an arrow in the torso; after that, it was overwhelmed and defeated.

The few wounded Seviathans left fled, because the combined forces of man and Stone Golem had proven too much. They retreated in all directions without a sense of unity or loyalty.

Gevnor met up with Lavrin and remarked, "I am glad to have such a mighty warrior as a son, but the people from the mining camp need a leader to direct them out of the Mazaron. They have decided I should be this leader."

Lavrin hugged his father and although it tore his heart apart, he answered, "I understand, Father. It seems we each have obligations. I know we will meet again, should the King grant us favor."

Father and son knelt together and prayed for each other. They lifted their pleas to the King, and hoped with all their hearts to one day find each other safe again.

The miners had found a distinct joy and love for Vin, which Lavrin had noticed. He did not want to sadden their hearts, so he let Vin travel with them. Lavrin then called to his litz, and it landed upon his hand. "Be their eyes and ears from the sky," he whispered to it. "Let no harm come to them, and make sure they are not discovered by the lizards." The litz took off into the sky.

Lavrin's father led the workers north, while Lavrin headed south with the Warriors of Light toward the heart of the Mazaron. Lavrin turned his head to watch his father disappear from view as they split paths. He knew it was the right thing to do, but nevertheless he felt part of his heart leave with them.

# CHAPTER 15

# BATTLE PLANS

Using the power of his evil arts, Natas transported himself into the Mazaron to the fortress where Jafer ruled. He needed to inspect the Seviathans before they were let loose to fight against the King's men to the north. Instantaneously, Natas appeared next to Jafer, who stood on the wall surveying the progression of his army. He wore his long dark purple robe and in his hand held the golden staff which ended in a large, sharp amethyst. This amethyst glowed with a purple aura. Jafer had a long scar along his arm and the same fierce yellow eyes which were characteristic of all Seviathans.

Natas murmured, "I see you are very intent on fulfilling your task."

Jafer turned with staff extended, expecting someone different. He then lowered his weapon and grumbled, "Why are you here? Do you not believe I can handle my own people?"

Natas' hand curled into a fist. "Sometimes, my minion, you forget your place with your arrogance. I want to see your army lined up in ranks for inspection." Jafer left Natas and delegated to his forces the things left to arm and train his militia.

The ranks were assembled; Natas scanned the creatures as he passed them by. While Jafer walked behind him, Natas corrected any flaw he found. Each lizard looked angry and aggressive, like a dog poked one too many times by its master.

Natas remembered the time of his first uprising against the King. He had corrupted the minds of a third of all the men and beasts in the Haven Realm, but was banished to Amcronos with his forces after being defeated. Natas then used his cunning wit and dark power to become ruler of Amcronos. Now the King was trying to reclaim the land once belonging to him.

Natas questioned Jafer, "Is every lizard armed?"

Jafer replied, "Yes, master."

Natas then asked, "Is every lizard trained?"

Jafer scoffed, "We have one hundred armed, trained and prepared Seviathans. They are ready to kill; we can begin the plan."

Natas proclaimed, "I want the Seviathans unleashed within the hour. I am needed elsewhere. Do not disappoint me, Jafer. You can always be replaced. Remember this is only phase one; if it does not succeed, you can be sure you will regret it. If the first wave of Seviathans does not defeat them, then the mission is lost." Natas vanished, leaving only a small pile of gray ashes in his place.

Jafer pointed his staff toward the gate. "You heard Natas! Go forth and show no mercy!" The mass flooded out of the gate and screamed a loud yell of bloodlust.

*****

Lord Auden and Lord Denethor neared the Mazaron Mountains with their troops, who now numbered four hundred twenty due to reinforcements from Srayo. Thankfully, Warren had commissioned some of the townsmen as extra guards so he was able to send twenty men to their aid. It was fortunate they had been able to capture the gang leader of Ken Van so quickly, and that his men had surrendered.

The warriors spied the vast mountains past a blanket of tree branches and gripped their weapons knowing that, although the scenery was breath-taking, it would bring forth a severe enemy. The Men of Light stopped at the foot of the mountains and set up formations. Auden and Denethor had decided to send scouts into the mountains two days ago to search for Seviathans, before venturing there themselves.

Auden and Denethor directed the soldiers to form a half moon in which the outside row would hold out their shields as a wall. The second row would be comprised of spear throwers. They would hopefully weaken the lizards before they reached the shield wall.

An unexpected exclamation rang out as the forces of the lords set up the half moon. "Men numbering in the seventies or eighties come from the Southwest. They are human, but wearing peasant clothing."

Both lords rushed toward the group with hope and anticipation that they were friendly and not an angry group of protestors. As they neared, they realized these were farmers. "Who goes there? Are you followers of the King of Light?"

They remarked, "We are farmers and sheep herders from the Island of Hessington, and we would gladly die for the King of Light a hundred times over. We were on our way to Srayo, since we heard of its liberation, but found you instead. We have come to serve under his banner against any foe. It has been too long since Hessington has had a say in the fight."

Denethor replied, "Praise the Light! We currently are readying to fight a battalion of Seviathans. They are cruel lizard men who have imprisoned the Mazaron Mountains. We would appreciate any possible help. We have extra weapons and armor for you to wear."

The Hessington civilians agreed to help them. Auden whispered to Denethor, "The small force we sent into the mountains needs our help, but we must train these farmers. They will greatly help our fight against the Seviathans."

The peasants were given the armor and weapons, and Auden, knowing they had little battle experience, began to train them intensely while Denethor planned a different strategy with their new numbers.

The peasants learned very quickly in the five days of training and did not struggle. Auden specifically focused their training on the front line to hold the wall of shields so that the experienced soldiers could fire arrows and jab with spears. The peasants were far from perfect at the start, but after hard work and patient teaching they became as knowledgeable as possible in the ways of war.

Denethor wondered if they would be ready for combat. He knew they were training well, but realized they lacked experience. Denethor did not wish these farmers to be wiped out by the oncoming threat. He was glad to have the men though, because with four hundred and ninety soldiers, hope was much closer for victory. The men from Hessington had the drive, but did they have the amount of strength necessary to battle the Seviathans?

# CHAPTER 16

# THE FORTRESS

With speed yet silence, Lavrin guided his group past large boulders and through various mountain paths and regions. A chilling breeze drifted through the damp air. Spots of grass sprouted through the soil, but trees were uncommon. The sun shone bright in the sky, but unfortunately was hindered by the mountainous fog. Rain clouds rolled in the distance past the mountains.

Kyra rubbed her arms to try to warm them and clutched them tightly to her body as she moved forward, staying close to Lavrin. Lavrin seemed undeterred by the cold, possibly due to his enthusiasm over finding his father after so many years. Although the weather did not favor them, the landscape was perfect for avoiding the watch of the Seviathans. Large stones lay in clusters, perfect for hiding behind, and the fog formed a veil atop them, further protection from enemy attention.

After treading through the unmarked lands of the mountains for an hour, the squad gazed upon a giant fortress. It backed up to the side of a mountain, and was surrounded by mountains to the right and the left.

The fortress was a shocking sight because it was completely red and black. This gave it a menacing appearance, as if to say, "I am unconquerable." A large black gate faced north and the walls of the fortress were loaded with catapults, trebuchets and archer towers.

Tathor declared, "Look at that. It is an army of hatred moving north with all speed." He pointed to a large army of one hundred Seviathans just below them, headed in the direction of Ken Van. Although they were hard to see from their altitude, it was obvious they were well-armed and planning to wreck havoc on the lands of Light.

Kyra stared in horror at the sight and leaned toward Lavrin. "If they reach Ken Van or Saberlin, all will be lost. I don't know if Auden and Denethor can stop that large of a Seviathan assault."

Lavrin turned his gaze back to the fortress. "If we can succeed in our mission, we could prevent that. All is not lost, but this tells us that if we do not act swiftly, the future will look very grim." Lavrin knew, as did all the others, that they could not even hope to attempt a frontal attack. Nor could they reach the fortress from any side without being spotted by the guards.

One soldier who had worked at the mining camp stepped up. He had small blue eyes, a thin frame, and scars running down his firm face and neck. "When I worked at the mining camp, I remember seeing a passage going deeper into the mountains. Often I would spot Seviathans traveling that direction. Sometimes I could hear them talking of a fortress, also."

Boranor agreed. "During my time pushing ore, I glimpsed a hole at the back of the camp and perceived it could head to the fortress. Yet it looked dangerous and uncertain so I had not told you of it earlier."

It appeared to be the best option for them, so Lavrin agreed they would take the secret tunnel route. It was a gamble, but since they had spied the force of Seviathans heading north, he suspected there would be few guards on the secret tunnel.

Along the return to the same tunnels where they had been, the group sped in haste to make up for lost time. Once, a soldier stopped when he heard a hissing noise coming from a shrub just beyond the pathway. He jumped backward in fright and instantaneously drew his sword. A gray rabbit hopped out from behind it, and the soldier sheathed his sword. His nearby comrades nudged him and laughed before continuing on the journey. Rowan made sure the rabbit was shot to be used for rations since as much supplies as possible would be needed.

When they reached the tunnel, Boranor did not enter it with them. They stopped and turned to him. Boranor remarked, "I cannot continue into the tunnels because I have other work to complete for the King of Light. I deeply wish I could come with you, but time is short and I know what I must do. I hope you can understand. This is a time for the Seviathans to be finished. I hope that we can meet again someday, and battle together against the ways of evil."

Lavrin nodded. "Go my friend. If you have something that burdens your heart to accomplish, then I will not stop you. Please do it with the King in mind, and I hope that you shall never forget us, as we will never forget you."

Many of the others were saddened and upset by Boranor's departure, but Lavrin knew that his motives were pure and that he had the King's best interests in mind. They started into the tunnels, past the run-down mining camp which was now abandoned and bare. Upon discovering a side of the rock wall carved out like a door, they praised the King for his fortune and set off.

# CHAPTER 17

# INTO THE DEPTHS

Entering the hole into the secret passageway, the first remark was from Rowan. “What is that putrid smell? It smells like rotten eggs and manure mixed with vinegar.”

Lavrin answered, “It is probably the smell of Seviathan.”

Kyra pondered, “How so?”

He explained. “Seviathans have most likely used these tunnels as a network between important places, much like the ones under Hightenmore, except for different uses. At Hightenmore, they were for storage and movement within the city in times of emergency. Although Seviathans could be using this for those purposes, I believe it is used rather for communication or for hiding, since lizards do dwell in dark places."

The group started slowly descending down the trail, shrouded in darkness and mystery. The torches they held sputtered weakly due to the lack of air, thereby illuminating little. Kasandra brushed spider webs off her face with disgust, and hoped that she would not encounter many more during this expedition.

Unlike the tunnels experienced beforehand, these were extremely narrow and had to be crossed in a single file line. Lavrin led the group with torch in hand and squinted to see the way in front of him. He slit his hand several times, trying to feel his way through the rocks. Many now understood that Boranor would have had to have departed anyway, since he would not have fit in these passageways.

Next in line after Lavrin, Kyra already wished to be out of the cramped pathway. However, she did not desire it nearly as much as Felloni wanted to return to the forest. He remembered the pure air and open land. He longed to run through the trees and taste the forest's variety of berries. Wet grass under bare feet and the amazing smell of the trees and plants were what he dreamed of longingly.

Truthfully, the forest was more of a home to Felloni than Gesloc, where he had been born and raised. To him it was one of the few peaceful places in Amcronos. He knew his loyalty to the King was far more important, though, than his preferences.

Their speed was slow, as it was difficult to maneuver in the tunnel system. Lavrin suddenly halted, causing everyone to bump into each other. He stared at a three-way fork ahead of him extending from a circular area. He stepped forward and allowed the others to squeeze their way around him.

He tried to see if one contained the scent of Seviathan stronger than another, but to no avail. He knew that although the one farthest right seemed to head closest in direction of the stronghold, it might have curved another way. Lavrin looked directly above the passageways and saw three symbols, one above each alley. One resembled a skull, one a snake, and the last a horse.

Kasandra exclaimed, "Look above!"

On the roof was carved:

**Follow your heart over your mind. Use speed in your movements but not in your decisions. Wait patiently to catch what you seek. This is the way that you succeed in survival. Let the colors of your banner display your character and your attributes.**

Lavrin read it once, then again. He processed the meaning of the text, knowing it was a riddle. "Follow your heart over your mind." He examined the symbols and determined it meant that since the skull held the mind, it was not the correct way. "Use speed in your movements, not in your decisions." Lavrin knew both snakes and horses moved with speed. Then, after rereading the other sentences, he began to understand. Both creatures survived by using patience, but only snakes caught their food for survival. Furthermore, snakes used their colors to describe their type like a banner would.

Lavrin began to head down the middle corridor marked with the snake. He was followed by the rest of his companions and friends. He was glad to find that no dead-ends or traps awaited them, although it was still hard to walk forward.

In order to keep up their energy along the way, everyone grabbed food out of their supplies and continued the struggle toward the heart of the enemy. Because time was racing, no stops were taken.

They now began to walk upward instead of downward. Lavrin urged them on constantly, insisting that speed was necessary to protect the King's lands in the Northwest of Amcronos.

Light came into view about ten minutes later from an arched doorway. The hearts of the squad rejoiced when they discovered they were right behind the fortress. Felloni told them to be silent. He spotted something which the others had not. The entrance into the fortress was guarded by four Seviathans. They were heavily armed with swords and stood as still as statues.

The doorway was outlined with carvings of eyes in a bronze border. Around this odd-looking border was nothing but harsh black rock. The rock jutted and spread in all directions except toward the entrance, as if fleeing from it. Occasional bits of gems could be seen, but were set deep within the tough stone. It was obvious that chunks of the rock had been hacked away because of several scrape markings.

Everyone understood that even if they fought and defeated the tall, bulky guards, the rest of the protectors would be alerted and would surround them, since only two thirds of the Seviathans had been sent out. Hearts dropped as they silently considered what they should do. Feet throbbed fiercely; all in all the team was exhausted. In their minds, they started to blame each other because of their frustration.

Suddenly, a loud crashing noise erupted in the direction of the Seviathan castle. The lizards guarding the entrance and all the defenders rushed to the front of their stronghold. Lavrin and the others snuck into the fortress when the lizard guards moved out, to find it all but open. Most the defenders were rushing toward the front wall.

The large front gate opened to reveal three Stone Golems pounding on the fortress by hurling large boulders. The Seviathans fired at them with all their armaments upon the wall. The three worked with precise unison, dodging the arrows and weapons while launching stones. Although most of the attacks were avoided, the golems were battered by the onslaught from the fortress as they tried to protect themselves.

One of the three bolted at the wall, mowing down some Seviathans along the way. The sneaking humans recognized the face of Boranor. He kicked one, smashed another, and then leapt upon the wall. Atop it, he focused on the trebuchets, catapults and other methods of defense. He snapped them into pieces like twigs, enduring pain from all sides intolerable to a human.

He landed upon one, crushing it beneath him, and then grabbed two Seviathans charging at him. Smashing their heads together, he tossed them aside. Knocking lizards off the wall, the Stone Golem seemed unharmed by the multiple attacks, but then began to stumble. The other two were also swarmed with Seviathans all over them, but continued to slam some off.

Meanwhile, the group of humans secretly edged their way toward what looked to be the lair of their leader. This lair was a building which extended partially out of the mountain. The outside had two stories; the top was a large balcony used to overlook the castle. It stood far higher from the ground than the first floor. The bottom story had no windows; it was mostly a curved wall with a single door to penetrate into it.

The group sprang upon unprepared Seviathans heading toward the front of the fortress. Suddenly, rain poured from the sky. Everyone was instantly blanketed in sheets of water. Chaos was thick within the fortress as Seviathans tried to battle the efforts of their opponents.

Felloni threw one of his knives into a Seviathan's stomach then Rowan shot an arrow between the eyes of the beast, defeating it within moments. Lavrin's dual swords met with those of a Seviathan. Lavrin knocked one out of its hand, stabbed the foe through its chest then spun to the side and jabbed his other sword into its back. After pulling them out, they were quickly cleansed of the blood by the heavy rain. He then dashed to catch up with his small yet effective fighting force.

Kasandra flung both of her spears in front of her at a tall Seviathan who skillfully flipped sideways, dodging both. Rowan shot it in the side, but that did not slow it down. Kasandra drew her other two spears to fight the creature which was preoccupied trying to claw through a round shield.

She ducked under its tail then jumped over another creature's hammer swing. Tathor knocked it off balance by hitting it with the back end of his axe. Kasandra seized this opportunity and sliced across the thick skin of its body with her spears. It did not survive the impact. Nearing the lair, Kyra turned her head to see the Stone Golems fighting for their lives; she knew in her heart that Boranor was one of those three, and he had known all along what needed to be done.

Boranor grabbed a thick board which had been broken off from a trebuchet and smashed everything in sight with it. He grabbed one Seviathan and pounded it into the wall, which knocked it out, and then launched the beast at a few others. When his club broke, Boranor jumped off the wall to make his attackers follow him.

Sadly, the golems were being overpowered by the sheer number of Seviathans who ripped with razor sharp claws at the hard cores of the golems' rocky flesh. Chunks of stone fell from their sides as their bodies began to shrink. The golems still had managed to hold them at bay and terminate as many as possible.

Using dwindling strength, the Stone Golems bashed and pounded their foes. They looked out for one another with surprising unity for those who had never fought together. When one was wounded or attacked, the other two came to his side and helped him battle. Still, numerous Seviathans remained to engage the enraged yet dying Stone Golems.

# CHAPTER 18

# THE ULTIMATE ENCOUNTER

Because Auden believed they were as prepared as possible, the training exercises were completed for the farmers of Hessington. Still, he wondered how strong of an enemy they were going to face. The scouts had just returned and reported that the Seviathan army was heading straight toward them and would be there in less than an hour. They numbered one hundred or so, and looked ready to kill anything in their path.

The lords knew they had to find a way to use their numbers to their advantage. Denethor thought of falling back into the forest, but that would help them little. Auden considered digging pits in which the creatures would fall, but they did not have the time for such a feat and it would tire out the men. One thing was for sure: they had to hold their ground. If they did not, the Seviathans would ravage through the lands of Amcronos loyal to the King.

"There must be some way to hold them off with the time we have remaining," Auden pondered.

Denethor knew he was right. They were the only hope of stopping the adversary. If these creatures were as fierce as they had been made out to be, the fight would be very hard to win. They needed some advantage that would turn the tide.

Auden suddenly jerked out of his train of thought and called to one of the soldiers from Dreylon, who came to him immediately. "Soldier," Auden asked him, "is not Ken Van a large holder of the North's horses?"

The soldier nodded. "Yes sir. They are mighty fine, too. They are not strong working horses like the ones raised in Dreylon, but they are awfully fast."

Auden knew this was the answer. If they were fast, they might arrive in time. Having a cavalry would be a huge asset. Auden had two horses which he and Denethor had ridden from Srayo. One was a tall chestnut horse with a white mane, freckled in white along the side. The other was as black as night from head to tail. They each had a large leather saddle which carried a bag of supplies and a few other necessities.

Auden quickly helped the soldier who he had questioned mount, along with one of his comrades, and sent them off. Auden knew that although they would not have enough horses for everyone in the army, it would give them a far better chance at defeating the Seviathans.

With all haste, the two zigzagged between trees and brush, as they felt the weight of the future of the Northwest on their shoulders. They would not stop, they could not rest, and no force in all Amcronos must delay them from reaching Ken Van. The horses snorted in protest at the intense speed at which they had to ride while dodging trees and other foliage. It was now a contest of who was more determined to finish first, Seviathans or humans.

It was highly fortunate that the horses had been well fed and rested so that they did not tire easily. They galloped rapidly, and as they neared a rapidly flowing stream, the riders forced them forward. The horses jumped across the stream majestically. The sound of their hooves created a methodic thundering as they crossed the forest.

When they broke free of the forest, Ken Van came into view. The thought on both warriors' minds was they needed to find the horses as quickly as possible. They exchanged their horses for new ones and headed to find Matthias. When they found him just after he had settled a large dispute, he helped them round up sixty excellent horses, understanding the men's urgency. The soldiers mounted their new rides, and with the help of thirty other men, they each held the reigns of their horse in one hand and the reigns of another horse in the other.

They started on the same route from which they had come, knowing that it was manageable. Guiding the multitude of horses was a challenge for them. They tried to travel swiftly but could not move nearly as fast as before. Eventually, they passed through the stream and knew that they were close. They hoped with all their hearts that they had not failed their army and their King.

Light began to stream into their eyes as they passed through the trees, and deep breaths of fresh air filled their lungs. No lizards, no death. They made it. The remaining horses were distributed to those chosen by the lords to form a cavalry. Those who had brought the horses made up most of it. Auden had decided that he would accompany the horsemen, but Denethor would be alongside those on foot.

For the moment they rested to regain their strength. The two lords had decided that the formation for the ground troops would consist of a spearhead, with the outside consisting of shield holders who also carried swords. The spears would all be given to the cavalry. Within the shield wall would be rows of archers ready to fire swiftly on the Seviathan brood.

The cavalry would wait until the Seviathans were out of the Mazaron, and then charge them in a striking run. They would run through as many as possible, then retreat back to the ground forces. After that, the archers would fire as many arrows as possible upon them before they reached the shield defense. Finally, after holding their ground for the archers as long as possible, the shield men would draw their swords and finish off the remainder with the rest of the horsemen.

The tall peaks of metal helmets rose from the army and the shield wall was formed. Large red and silver shields, almost as tall as a man, lined the two diagonal rows. The archers, with eyes like falcons, surveyed the grand mountain scene and caressed the feather ends of their arrows. A breeze washed over them and daunting black clouds rolled overhead.

Hearing a deafening screech, the soldiers' eyes all darted to the mountains where a multitude of Seviathans flocked toward them. Many of the soldiers trembled with fear at the sight of the mighty enemy before them. The lizards bounded from the mountains with incredible haste. Auden mounted his new steed and, seeing the terror displayed in the men, called forth, "The great King of Light, may he live and reign forever, and may his followers prosper!"

They rallied together, replying, "The great King of Light, may he live and reign forever, and may his followers prosper!"

Again Auden declared, "The great King of Light, may he live and reign forever, and may his followers prosper!"

Once more the men cried forth, "The great King of Light, may he live and reign forever, and may his followers prosper!"

The ranks were tightened, and after waiting until the beasts reached the foot of the mountains, the cavalry rode off to face them. Rain began to pour down so hard it seemed unnatural. This did not deter either side.

Denethor prepared his ground forces for battle which would occur after the horsemen had done their damage. Auden and his men held their spears with valor and charged into the Seviathan army. Seviathans leapt upon the horses with vengeance, but the riders struck many of them down with the sharp tips of their long spears.

While some Seviathans fell, others cleverly avoided the spear thrusts, then struck the horses and riders. The Riders of Light used an advanced crossing pattern. One row of riders attacked the Seviathans who were following the row in front of them. Meanwhile a different row of horsemen would thrust into those following the row in front of them. This left the enemy confused and vulnerable. The Seviathans though, were smarter than anticipated, and sneakily charged at the enemy when weak, anticipating their strike.

One lizard dove toward Auden, who reared his horse to avoid it. He then drove his spear through the lizard. Sadly, though, another lizard had knocked a nearby rider off with an arrow to the shoulder. Auden had tried to circle around to recover him, but he was not to be found.

Auden yelled to his warriors, "Retreat to the ground forces!" They heard it immediately and turned back. Auden trampled over one Seviathan while he retreated with his horse, and then led the thirty other men who had survived back to the triangle of ground troops.

The Seviathans dashed toward them with surprising speed after being wounded by the first attack. The large shields were held up by the crouching soldiers at the same time as the archers drew back their longbows. Some of them were armed with the new technology of powerful crossbows.

Denethor gave the signal and an onslaught of arrows was fired. The lizards were hit by some of the arrows, but many others missed them. Although some Seviathans fell dead from the blast, it was not as many as hoped for. Now it all rested on the strength of the blockade of shields to buy more time for the archers.

Crash! Seviathan metal banged and clashed into human defenses. Another volley of arrows was fired into the beasts before the Seviathans broke through the wall. It was now the lizard men's turn to repay the damage.

The Forces of Light dispersed under the rampage of the creatures. Even while damaged and bruised, the lizard men killed on with a furious offensive. It seemed now not a battle, but a crazy frenzy which erupted in every direction. Formation had been broken and, as the lords tried to regain control, the battle continued in torment.

# CHAPTER 19

# FINAL STRUGGLE

Valiantly, Boranor fought on with a rage stronger than that of the Seviathans who opposed him outside the fortress. He fought for his kind, he fought for his life. Most of all, he fought for his King. This was his time to repay all the hardships put upon him for many years. No more would he hibernate within the mountains; he would fight no matter the cost.

Against all odds, he plowed down his opponents while his body was being ripped apart. Whenever he attacked or swung one direction, he was wounded from the other. Not the hardest of stone could have endured this torture forever, and Boranor began to crumble.

Realizing this, he knew he needed to survive just a little longer to buy more time for his small but loyal human friends.

He bashed into the horde of Seviathans that were pilling on top of his fellow kin. This freed them from their pain for the moment. The three fought side by side, crushing and pounding, smashing and knocking lizards left and right.

Miserably, this was harder than expected, for the Seviathans seemed to have an undefeatable will to survive. Although many were killed, many others withstood numerous attacks and kept on battling. Pain rushed nonstop up the golem's nerves of steel and almost finished them.

*****

Tathor bashed through the door which led into Jafer's lair. Lavrin instructed Tathor and most of the team to guard and barricade the door and allow no Seviathans to follow them in. Lavrin, Felloni, Kasandra, Rowan and Kyra continued toward the main throne room where they expected the Seviathan King to be. They entered it to find Jafer seated on his golden throne, with two large brute guards beside him. On the cavernous walls were displays of precious stones and prized artifacts of gold, silver and bronze. Countless torches aligned them, giving a sparkling effect like the sun on a pool of water.

Jafer laughed in a sinister tone. "You fools! You think that five humans can defeat the King of the Seviathans with his two best warriors?"

Lavrin answered, "We have the power of the King on our side and can overcome Natas himself, you cockroach of evil!"

Jafer stood and snarled, "Prove it! Guards, kill them!"

Tathor ran into the room. "They have it handled. I will help you defeat this puny king." They nodded to each other, ready for the fight. They knew they did not have the best of odds, and to succeed they must work as a team.

Everyone held their weapons with poise and zeal. The two Seviathans guards looked like the lizard who had confronted Felloni and Tathor when finding the Perifern, but were wiser in the ways of battle. Both of Jafer's defenders carried a spiked chain mace in one hand, and a broad scimitar in the other. They wore crystal necklaces like the others, yet they were slightly larger and tougher.

Felloni and Lavrin moved toward one, while Kasandra and Tathor faced the other. Rowan drew an arrow, knelt and aimed toward Jafer. Kyra secretly crept out of the room and through a side door with hopes to ambush Jafer from behind.

Lavrin deeply wished they could have the aid of the Stone Golems against their foes, but he knew they were buying time for them to defeat Jafer. Lavrin held his swords firmly as he and Felloni fought the guard from both sides. Loud bangs erupted from the heavy pounding on the door into the lair. The soldiers braced it with all their might, but they could not hold long.

Felloni ducked under a mace attack but the Seviathan dodged his knife slice to the right. Lavrin knocked the scimitar out of its hand, but it hastily recovered it and blocked a downward blow from Lavrin. Lavrin tried to stab the brute in the leg, but it dodged and bit him in the arm. As Lavrin reeled in pain, Felloni side-kicked the creature, spun and slammed a knife into its lower back, then rolled in front of it and sprang into an uppercut. It retaliated with a jab with the back of its sword across his face.

Rowan launched arrows at Jafer, but he slid and spun out of their way. Jafer then held out his staff and blasted Rowan with a powerful ray which came from the dark power through the crystal at the end of it. As Rowan flew backwards and crashed into the wall, he knew they would have trouble trying to defeat a wielder of such rare and powerful weapons. He moaned in pain from the impact.

Kasandra soared behind her foe by leaping off the back of Tathor. She locked its neck and Tathor inserted both axes into its sides with a downward motion. The creature knocked Kasandra off with a swing of his mace then pinned Tathor's hand to the wall with its tail. Tathor, however, used his other hand to elbow it in the jaw. Kasandra launched a spear at it from behind. It collapsed to the ground lifeless, and Tathor kicked it off his body.

Kasandra glanced behind her and spied Rowan getting up from the floor. Tathor whipped his axe into the air directly toward Jafer, but he deflected it back at him. Tathor was impacted instantly by the reflected weapon which cut into his left leg, since he had never expected it to be turned against him.

The Seviathans slammed a battering ram into the door and its impact sent some of the men flying backward. They rushed back to their post but the door was splintered.

Rowan was about to shoot another arrow at Jafer, but seeing what had happened to Tathor, did not. They needed another approach. Lavrin and Felloni still brawled with the other guardian. It kicked Felloni aside with power, and then twirled its mace at Lavrin. Lavrin blocked it, but then was scored in the chest with the scimitar. Thankfully, it was barely deep enough to pierce the armor, or it would have done serious damage.

The Seviathan opened its mouth to bite Lavrin again, but this time in the neck. It then stumbled backward in agony when an arrow, shot by Rowan, pierced one of its eyes. Felloni saw it was weak and lunged at it, killing it with several knife sweeps. Meanwhile, Kasandra tried to endure numerous staff blasts but was hurled across the room like a rag doll by Jafer. Rowan was the next victim, and again was thrown into the back wall.

Jafer suddenly roared. Kyra had jabbed her knife into his shoulder from behind. She yelled, "Take that, beast!" Jafer turned and, conjuring up an ice wind, froze her to the wall.

Rowan then directed two arrows into his arm, causing Jafer to drop the staff. Lavrin sprinted toward it, rolled to the left and inserted his blade into Jafer's heart. He shrieked an ear-piercing scream and collapsed onto the floor. Hearing their master was dead, the Seviathans crashed into the lair. Those trying to protect the entrance retreated deeper within, but were overwhelmed.

Lavrin picked up the staff. Kasandra exclaimed, "Destroy it!"

He countered, "No, we can use it against them!"

Suddenly he dropped the staff and fell to his knees, realizing the roaring pain in his arm. Rowan picked up the staff and, seeing the Seviathans berserk with frustration, smashed it into the ground. Unexpectedly, he was inflicted with an arrow strike to the chest just as he destroyed it. The lizard men oddly began to flee out of the lair instead of continuing the assailment. Their necklaces seemed to slowly lose their glow due to the destruction of the staff. Kyra's snare quickly melted to a pool of water. She gasped for breath, and then sighed with relief.

Outside the lair, lightning rippled from the sky and the moon grew crimson red, like the color of the blood spilled that day. The thunder which accompanied the nonstop peals of lightning sounded like the explosion of a volcano. The sky was lit up by the flashing streaks and became an awe-inspiring sight to behold.

Kyra knelt beside Rowan. Frantically, she tried to limit the flow of blood and restart his failing heart. Hitting his chest with her fist, she could not help his heart beat again. She worked to no avail and could not keep him alive for long. He whispered, "Do not...worry...about me. We won...the day." His spirit soon left his body, and made its way toward the Haven Realm.

With tears in her eyes, Kyra rushed to help Tathor, who suffered the severe leg injury from his own axe, and also those who were injured defending the entrance. Kasandra collapsed upon her friend's body and cried, "Rowan, no! Rowan, don't leave me!"

She tried to wipe the tears away but to no avail. Felloni sat next to her and tried to comfort her. "It's okay to cry. Always remember that Rowan died an honorable death."

She sputtered, "I can't believe he is dead."

Trying to soothe her grieving heart, Felloni replied, "I don't know all the plans of the King, but I know he had a plan for calling Rowan into the Haven Realm."

# CHAPTER 20

# REUNION AND REESTABLISHMENT

At the foot of the Mazaron Mountains, as the army led by the lords fought the brutal Seviathan invasion, the enemies of the King suddenly stopped battling as if dazed or in a trance. Auden called off the fight when the Seviathans began to run off in paralyzed fear. Some of them, though, were captured by the lords' men and were bound with rope securely.

Cheers arose from the army, and Auden and Denethor both knew within their hearts that it was due to the victory of Lavrin and the special group. It was only by the King's might that it had happened this way, because the end had been near and their backs had been pushed to the edge of the forest. The

Seviathans had penetrated deep into the army and had almost separated the group completely. The army looked up to the sky as it rippled and flashed brilliantly. They noticed the necklaces of the Seviathans were now dull and losing their glow.

While this was happening, a small band appeared from the mountains and headed toward them. With looks of relief and joy on their tired faces, they exclaimed, "We have been freed from a mining camp in the Mazaron by an elite group of warriors several days prior."

Auden and Denethor replied, "We sent that force as a secretive attack squad against the Seviathans. It seems they have completed their mission."

Gevnor stepped forward. "I am the leader of this group and the father of Lavrin. Thanks to the King, I have once again been reunited with my long lost son."

*****

Back at the fortress, Lavrin stared at the sky's peculiar, incredible state. "That was no ordinary staff to cause the sky to peel with lightning and to make the moon turn as red as the wings of a robin."

Felloni entered the jail and freed the prisoners. He recognized some of them from the refugee camp. Normad, the father of Margret and Eli, told him that some of the prisoners had come to trust in the ways of the King. Felloni led all of those imprisoned to the rest of the group. Many were reunited with those they had known before the Seviathan assault of the refugee camp. Lavrin handed the horn from the camp to

Normad. He took it sadly, knowing this meant that their leader was dead, yet was appreciative of the kind gesture.

The main army soon met with their elite force in the fortress while the rain slowed to a sprinkle. They congratulated them on their victory and recounted the battles together. A brilliant rainbow shone in the sky and its pure colors were a sight to behold.

At the same time, Idrellon landed in the once Seviathan castle carrying a bag filled with intricate silver bands. These bands were distributed to the captured Seviathans, and wondrously allowed them to speak and understand the human tongue. The bands had some unique writing engraved across them which the humans could not read. Circular yellow gems were in each center, surrounded by rings of silver. These made them look just like the eyes of a Seviathan.

The lizards were questioned for their actions in a large assembly. They told those gathered there, "We could not control our own minds. The staff used by Jafer had trapped us to the necklaces. As it imprisoned our minds, we watched ourselves kill the innocent, but we could not fight the power which enslaved us. When it was destroyed, we were free from his control."

Everyone opened their mouths in shock. Was it true? They had been controlled the whole time? Auden stammered, "So, you mean to say that just as you imprisoned the villagers, Jafer had imprisoned you through his staff for all these years?"

They hung their heads in shame. "That is exactly what happened. We could not have conceived that when we were formed into the Seviathan army, taking a necklace as a sign of our allegiance would result in the imprisonment of our own minds."

After this shocking knowledge, Lavrin and Felloni questioned Idrellon if he had heard of such a thing. Not even he knew of such a staff. Lavrin asked, "What of our departed friends? Do they fair well?"

He replied, "They have been watching you this whole time and are enjoying a perfect, painless life in the Haven Realm. They have discovered many truths which cannot be understood here. The things most desirable here are but a vapor compared to the vast glory of the Haven Realm."

"Why did Macrollo, the talking leopard warrior, not need a silver band like the Seviathans do?" asked Felloni.

Idrellon stated, "He needed one at first as I did, but we steadily learned how to talk without them."

Lavrin and Felloni left Idrellon and began to help with the dead. They were gathered into a large pile on top of a stack of wood, and burned. The Seviathan necklaces were also burned to ensure they would never again be used. Sweat caked upon the Men of Light's faces, but they cared little since they had won against the evil schemes of Jafer.

Lord Auden and Lord Denethor talked as they walked toward the King's scribe. Auden pondered, "My dear friend, shall we return to our homes?"

Denethor looked to the north longingly. "Yes, we will. I believe it would be best if you rule Hightenmore and Ken Van while I take Saberlin and my home of Vanswick. Then we shall give Dreylon to Warren to govern as well. I believe he will learn quickly and we can always aid him in times of confusion or trouble."

Auden approved. He turned to talk with Idrellon. "So who will govern the Mazaron?"

Idrellon remarked for all to hear, "The Stone Golems shall sleep no more. They shall rule these mountains as they had for many years in the past."

While Boranor and the other two Stone Golems approached, Idrellon proclaimed, "I, as ambassador and scribe of the King of Light, hereby decree that the age of Seviathans has passed away, and the reign of Stone Golems will once more occur throughout the Mazaron. Boranor shall be at the head of this rule."

Although all the men cheered, Boranor was deeply humbled. "It is a great honor. I hope I will use wise judgment to oversee these rocky lands."

Boranor and the other two Stone Golems let out a load roar that echoed through the mountains. Rising up out of the ground, Stone Golems began to appear near the fortress. Boranor was grieved to find that only twenty of his kind had survived, but knew that things would only get better in times to come. Cheers ensued by the Men of Light, knowing the cruel slavery within the Mazaron had been finished.

Lavrin turned his head and did not see Kyra anywhere. He then became nervous and rushed through the fortress, calling out, "Kyra? Where are you, Kyra?"

Rushing to and fro, Lavrin began to fear the worst, until Kyra eventually called out, "I'm here Lavrin." He turned around and saw her behind him. "I just had to finish healing the wounded."

Lavrin hugged her. "When I could not find you, I feared ill had happened to you; it made me realize that I could not live without you." Kyra's heart pounded heavily in agreement, and she could not speak because of the large lump in her throat.

Lavrin and Kyra then met up with Felloni and Kasandra. Kasandra told Lavrin, Kyra and Felloni that she wished to join the three of them in whatever adventures further awaited them in Amcronos.

A Seviathan with a silver band across his arm and a longbow strapped to his back rushed up in front of Kasandra, and fell to his knees with head bowed. He muttered, "I, I, I am the one who killed your friend. I am so sorry. Could you ever forgive me?" Kasandra instinctively grabbed one of her spears and was about to attack the Seviathan when Felloni whispered to her, "What would Rowan have wanted?"

She loosened her grip and stammered, "What is your name?"

The lizard man answered, "Uminos."

Kasandra continued, "Did you have control over your body when you killed him?"

"The crystal was just too strong for me."

Kasandra looked Uminos in the eyes. "Then I forgive you."

Uminos stood up and said, "I pledge to be your slave and to obey you, protect you and follow you."

Kasandra was taken back. "If you truly wish to accompany me, I want you as a bodyguard or ally, but not as a slave."

Uminos replied, "I understand. I will accompany you and your friends, and serve the Light even if it costs me my life, for I have never encountered anyone with such mercy toward me."

The lords, along with the Seviathans, fighters and liberated prisoners, headed north toward Ken Van. Denethor carried both the copy of the King's histories and the staff with the broken end which once belonged to Jafer. He would display them in Vanswick, and hoped to add this adventure to the King's histories with Matthais' approval.

The Seviathans chose to dwell in the refugee camp where they could stay in contact but not be observed by the townsfolk. Understandably, they did not desire to raise terror or endure mockery from the village folk, so they felt the refugee camp would be an excellent home for them, since it resembled their life in the caves.

The five decided to stay in the mountains and help convert the villages to the ways and truth of the King. Lavrin promised his father he would head north soon and meet him in Saberlin. Amcronos would now become much more loyal to the Light than ever before with the addition of the Mazaron. It would take time to ease the troubled and stressed hearts of the villages, but the five believed that, with the hope, peace, and the love of the King, all things were possible. Nevertheless, the rest of Amcronos was far more stubborn and evil; they would not join the ways of Light so easily.

# AFTERWORD

Natas stared through the smokescreen that allowed him to view all of Amcronos. He witnessed the collapse of Jafer and the freedom of the Seviathans, villages and the Mazaron Mountains as a whole.

Angrily, he overturned the nearby table, spilling ink and scattering papers and books in every direction. The table clashed onto a large pot, smashing it into shards. It was as if steam actually rose out of Natas' ears due to the thick anger within him. "Those idiots!" Suddenly he stopped dead in his tracks. A thought entered in his head. A devious smile accompanied a sinister laugh. "They think they have won by defeating a small portion of my army? What they don't know is that I perceive each and every weakness in them. Now let's see if they can withstand being broken apart through their emotions. It is time to unleash the…"

# AUTHOR'S NOTE

The King served by the Forces of Light represents Jesus Christ. Just as they trusted in the goodness of the King, you can believe in the holiness of God. You do not need to say any special words, just believe in your heart Jesus Christ is the Son of God and know he died for your sins. You may say, "I don't have any sins, though." Or, "I don't need God." Have you ever cheated, even if only once? Have you ever disobeyed your parents? These are just two of several types of sins. These sins will cast you into the endless fires of Hell when you die.

Thankfully, Jesus Christ died on the cross to cover our transgressions. His blood can cover your sins and make you as white as snow. Please understand this does not mean your life will become perfect and there will be no more pain. However, it will give you the assurance of a brighter future that, just like Rowan entered the Haven Realm, we will travel to Heaven after we die. It will be a place of unfathomable things, like roads of gold and gates of pearls. No pain will accompany us there and sorrow will be but a thing of the past.

If you have already accepted the reality of God and have dedicated yourself to his will for you, I am thankful for this. I encourage you to read the Bible because it is a book like no other and can strengthen your faith tremendously.

Fight the good fight and stand against the forces of the devil. As Lavrin and his comrades overcame their struggles against the Seviathans, you can also defeat the sin in your life, and by doing so affect your church, community, and possibly the world! Never stop pursuing your dreams and make sure that whatever you do, you do it for God's glory. God bless. The great King of Light, may he live and reign forever, and may his followers prosper!